CAL'S MISSION

VICTIM'S JUSTICE

Richard M Beloin MD

authorHOUSE®

AuthorHouse™
1663 Liberty Drive
Bloomington, IN 47403
www.authorhouse.com
Phone: 1 (800) 839-8640

Published by AuthorHouse 04/12/2019

ISBN: 978-1-7283-0783-1 (sc)
ISBN: 978-1-7283-0782-4 (e)

DEDICATION

This Western Fiction is dedicated to my children—David, Dennis and Lise.

CONTENTS

PROLOGUE

Amos Farley and Cal Harnell were hot on the trail of the well-known Hasting's gang. They had been tracking them for six days and finally set their eyes on the gang some four hundred yards away. With the use of their 50X binocular telescope, they could tell that the gang's horses were at a walk and looked spent. They elected to push their fresh horses to a full gallop, to catch up with the gang, and force them into a decisive confrontation.

Meanwhile, Omer Hasting was checking his back trail when he noticed a dust cloud and two riders at a full gallop. He yells to his men, "we have a tail coming at us. Our horses are spent, and we can't outrun them. So, let's go in this small canyon and set up a defense."

Amos saw the gang heading for a canyon and said, "Cal, they're entering that canyon and it's a dead end. Their going to look for a defensive spot and start shooting." They followed the gang, and when the gang saw that it was a dead end, they veered to the right and headed for large rocks next to the canyon wall. Amos and Cal reacted, went to the opposite side and set up behind protective boulders. Amos says to Cal, "I'll shoot at them to give you cover, while you get the horses behind protective boulders." Cal came back with his Winchester 1876.

His rifle had a Malcolm 8X telescope installed to compensate for his lifelong poor vision. He had "old man's eyes" and could not see the front sight of his rifle. This scope allowed him to hit a man size target at 400-450 yards, or a quarter mile, which was the limit of a 45-90 cartridge in a carbine length barrel.

Amos then says, "we are approximately 350 yards away from those scoundrels. Unless they have a long-range rifle like you do, their 1873 rifles in 44-40 won't be accurate. Set your scope at 400 yards since the elevation is over 6000 feet—which adds an extra 50 yards to your actual distance." Cal made the elevation adjustments and the shooting began.

Meanwhile Omer Hastings says to his men, "we made a mistake taking refuge this far from the other canyon wall, so shoot high since your shot will fall low." His Segundo, Slim Duval, adds, "we didn't have much choice since this yardage is the same throughout the canyon. Let's hope that these bounty hunters don't have a long-range rifle." As he finished talking, a bullet hit the outlaw next to the Segundo and blew off the back of his head. Omer yells out, "they've got a long-range. rifle, so keep your heads down. We'll slip out of here when darkness falls."

Amos continued firing with his rifle, trying to goad them to stick their heads up to fire, but they weren't buying it. Amos says, "Cal, get ready, I'm going to lift my hat on a stick and that will draw one up." As expected, an outlaw peeped up and Cal hit him in the upper chest. That was the last time they fell for that trick.

Cal asked Amos what their plan should be to end this standoff. "Sometime after midnight, this gang will make a run for it when they expect us to be asleep. Fortunately, this is a moonless night and after dark, take your sawed-off shotgun and sneak up to their left flank. When they start getting ready to leave, pop up and give them both barrels of #3 buckshot. Remember, these are violent murderers that have been given the option to surrender. Don't give them a second chance because you will not survive the confrontation."

Cal took his leather pouch holding a charcoal chunk and blackened his face and hands. That along with all black clothing made him an inconspicuous shadow in the night. He moved to his far right and then covered the 350 yards to the rock array next to the canyon wall. He then sneaked to the gang's location and got to within fifteen yards of them.

He waited till they were getting ready to leave. When Omer instructed Slim to get the horses, Cal stood up and said, "lift your hands and give up or you're dead." In total disbelief, the gang's uniform response was to draw their pistols. Cal let go both barrels and three of the outlaws dropped to the ground. Omer had been hit, but still was able to draw his pistol.

Cal outdrew him and shot him in the chest with a fatal wound.

Amos came over and they scavenged the six dead outlaws. Their pockets had a total of $389 which they split up. The saddlebags had the usual boxes of 44-40 ammo, food and extra clothing. The big find was Omer's saddlebags containing $4000 of greenbacks. They pocketed the shared funds, loaded the outlaws on their saddles and gathered all the guns.

After daylight, they cooked a hot breakfast of bacon, home fries, beans, hoecakes and a lot of coffee. Amos took the opportunity to breach a subject he had been putting off. "Cal, I'm sixty years old and it's time to retire from this dangerous profession. You may never have realized why I took you on as a greenhorn a year ago. There were two reasons. The first was to train my replacement with the tools that gave me the ability to survive as a bounty hunter. The second was because I was getting too old to keep up with the physical demands. So, in return for giving you the tips of the trade, you did all the heavy work and took all the risks, like you did last night."

Amos continued after a pause, "Cal, this is my last bounty hunting event. I've been lucky to have survived the past fifteen years. For years I made a living as a bounty hunter but only this past year have I been able to put money aside. That's because we undertook some bad gangs like this Hasting gang with $6,000 worth of rewards. In the past year I have put away $50,000. At our distribution of 75—25%, I expect you have also banked at least $16,000. With my account I can buy a small house in town and get a part time job to supplement my interest income. You have seed money to get a business started and settle down with a wife."

"What if I wanted to continue being a bounty hunter, do you have any recommendations?" "Yes, don't go solo, get a partner or a cur dog. If you go solo, you'll be hunting minor criminals that have low rewards. With a dog you can go after one or two more dangerous outlaws, and with a partner you can go after gangs like we've done all year. Either way, a dog or partner both need training."

So, they got on the trail heading back to Montrose, to claim their rewards, after a lawman identified the bodies. After a few miles, Cal found himself woolgathering and recalled the last year's events that brought him to this day.

It all started when Cal was eighteen and his parents passed away. His mother died of pneumonia and his father died in a silver mine accident. Cal wanted to work and tried several professions. Ranching was not for him, he couldn't see spending all day in the saddle chasing cows. So, he tried jobs in town. He could not handle the customers that a mercantile worker had to serve. He tried blacksmithing but could not get enthused pounding metals all day. Finally, he went to work as an apprentice in a gun shop. This was a winner. He learned how to repair guns and do action jobs. He ended up with free housing when the owner got married and moved out of the rear living quarters. He had a kitchen, heat stove and bed. In return, he provided nighttime security and still made $1 a day.

The best part of this gunsmith job was the cheap ammo he was allowed, 30 cents a box of 50 rounds compared to the retail price of 50 cents per box. The gunsmith showed him how to properly perform a fast draw and Cal practiced the fast draw three times a day and shot 25 rounds daily for a whole year. The gunsmith knew he was proficient when Cal was able to master this test. Cal took a pint size tin can with one inch of dirt and dropped it off his left hand from waist high. Cal could fast draw, shoot, and hit it twice before the tin can hit the ground.

After two pleasant years of gun shop employment, Cal had an encounter with Amos Farley. One day Amos arrived at the sheriff's office with a manacled prisoner. Cal was listening at the sheriff saying that this outlaw had a wanted poster worth $750. Cal was taken up with the value of the outlaw. He finally got the nerve to address the bounty hunter. For reasons that Cal never understood, the bounty hunter was cordial and talked extensively with Cal. Eventually Cal asked Amos for a job. Amos asked what he had for qualifications. Cal said he had mastered the *fast draw. When Cal gave a demonstration, he was hired on the spot.*

Continuing on the trail, Cal came back to reality and asked Amos where he planned to settle down in retirement. He said, "I have my only brother, his wife and three kids plus all the grand nephews and nieces that live in a small railroad town called Silver Circle, some forty miles from Pueblo, Colorado. Several family members work at the W—M Connected Ranch. This is a crop farming enterprise owned and operated by a well-known retired bounty hunter, by the name of Wayne Swanson. I'll apply for a job and if I like it, I'll buy a small house in town."

"What about you Cal?" "I guess I'll go on my own for now and look for the easier jobs." "If you think of getting more advanced in your manhunts, start thinking of hooking up with a lawman sponsor who can guide you to the active outlaws in your area or state. As a matter of fact, here's a list of suggestions from my past experiences:"

1. "Whenever you arrive in a new town, stop and visit with the town's lawman. Go over the posters of wanted men and check to see if there is a recent sighting or activity of the men you are hunting."
2. "Don't go on a manhunt if you don't have the last location that the outlaw has been seen. Blind traveling is usually nonproductive."
3. "Use the telegraph freely. Communicate with your sponsor or other lawmen in outlying communities. Every bit of information is useful."
4. "Always be safe and never take unnecessary chances. Especially when entering a room or setting up camp for the night."
5. "When tracking an outlaw, use every track's unique identifying feature. Don't try to ride too fast and end up losing the trail."

"You're at the peak of your game as far as having the ability to perform this dangerous profession. I caution you to not get involved with a woman when you are on manhunts. These are times that you need your total attention and there is no room for woolgathering and personal involvements. If you fall in love, it's time to start thinking of changing professions because it is not fair to the woman or to you."

"Well this brings up two subjects that I'm interested in. This idea of a dog as a partner and what modern avenue does a bounty hunter have for the future?"

"Let's talk about a trained dog. A dog can assist you in dealing with a confrontation by attacking one of the outlaws and taking him out of the fight. He can scare an outlaw into divulging some bit of information you need. He will warn you of an intruder entering your camp while you are asleep. Dogs have a sixth sense and can warn you of an impending ambush or drygulching. The advantages are endless as well as providing companionship on the road. The drawbacks are that the dog needs to be fed and cannot travel 40 miles a day like a horse can. I once saw a packsaddle modified to still carry two panniers but having a platform with low walls that fit between the two sides of the packsaddle. It really looked funny to see the dog riding on the packhorse's platform, but it worked. The other drawback is the training involved, and of course, the smarter the dog, the shorter is the learning curve."

"The other issue is whether there is a long-term future in bounty hunting. My dream was that I would eventually start a bounty hunting business like the Pinkertons have started in Denver. I always believed in the old saying, 'see one, do one, teach one.' In short, you can always start a free school to teach the art of safe bounty hunting. Then send out teams of two hunters after criminals and share the bounty with them. As the business owner and instructor, it allows you to settle down and start a family. This can be your long-term goal."

They finally arrived in Montrose and went directly to the sheriff's office. The bodies were identified by the sheriff and he offered to notify the agencies who posted the rewards. The Western Union vouchers would arrive within two days. They also sold the six outlaw horses with full tack for $420, the six colts for $150, the six 1873 rifles for $250, and the two shotguns for $60. The grand total was $880 plus the $6,000 bounty and the $4,000 from Omer's saddlebags.

Amos and Cal spent three leisurely days waiting for the vouchers. They had a long visit at the tonsorial shop to get a shave, haircut and hot bath. After their baths, they changed into new clothes. They enjoyed a few beers and friendly card games at the local saloons. Meals in the local diner were always a delight compared to food on the trail. The most pleasant thing was sleeping on a real bed for three nights in a row.

During the three days, Amos took the opportunity to buy new clothing and footwear for town living and working on a crop farm. Whereas, Cal bought camouflaged bounty hunter clothing in black, dark grey or dark blue. Cal also had the local hostler/farrier shoe his two horses, Boss and Buster, and replace some of the worn tack. Amos gave Cal all his equipment to include: packhorse, packsaddle, panniers, hatchet, spade, cooking equipment and utensils, fire grate, bandages, carbolic acid and sewing kit.

The day of departure, Amos bought a ticket for himself to Silver Circle, some 200 miles east. Cal was going to do the same, but when he heard the railroad ticket teller mention the several train yard robberies in Salida, Cal changed his destination to Salida, some 100 miles east of Montrose and half way to Silver Circle.

Little did Cal realize that this stop in Salida was the beginning of his lifelong mission—to provide some degree of justice for victims of violent crimes.

***

CHAPTER 1—Saving Max

The train arrived in Salida three hours later. Cal said his goodbyes to Amos but made it clear they would stay in touch by telegraph for the next year. Cal picked up his two horses and tied them up to the hitching rail. He spent some time talking to the railroad yard agent. Apparently, the special car carrying gold bars from the smelter, and large amounts of cash, was held up 10 days ago. This was carried out by the Spencer gang, a well-known outlaw gang throughout the state.

Cal asked, "what did they get away with?" The agent said, "they blew off the car's door. The concussion knocked out the two guards. They could not unlock the large Mosler safe to get the cash, but they filled their saddlebags with gold bars. The railroad detectives reported that the four outlaws carried some 40 pounds per saddlebags, or at least 160 pounds. At the current rate of $20 per ounce, we are talking about a $50,000 heist."

"This is a big loss for the railroad and it's not covered by insurance. The railroad has placed a $10,000 reward for the return of the gold and all four outlaws. The railroad detectives gave chase but lost the trail after the gang separated to parts unknown in a dense forest." Cal thought, *that was a stupid and poorly planned robbery. By knocking out the guards, there was no one to open the safe. So, out of desperation and the need to escape, they quickly picked up some gold bars. What were they thinking? Did they expect to go to a bank and exchange a three-pound gold bar for $1,000 in cash. What idiots! I bet that they did not go far, and will be back in a week or two, to rob the bank that had the cash delivery that day.*

Cal figured he had plenty of time waiting for the Spencer gang. He brought his horses to the local livery, took a hotel room and decided to take it easy till the gang showed their heads. After a few days in town, several people told him that he should visit a hot spring. One day he got Boss and took a ride to the nearest hot spring. The people in the hot pool said that the water temperature was 102 to 108 degrees. Cal changed in an old pair of britches cut off above the knees. He walked slowly into the hot pool and after getting use to the stink of rotten eggs, he finally settled down. He soaked in the pool for a half hour, but had to step out for a while, because he was getting dizzy. Yet, he returned several times back in the water.

Eventually, he decided to pay 50 cents to be able to rinse in warm fresh water, before getting back in his regular clothes, and throwing away the cut-off britches. Cal was curious how the attendant controlled the water temperature. He answered, "the natural water temperature is in the 150-degree range. I add cold fresh water from a nearby stream and the mix is kept in the hot but safe range."

Cal enjoyed his day and headed back to Salida. He was planning to go to a dog fight that evening. This was another event, like the hot springs, that were well advertised by the local residents. Although he had misgivings about such a sport, he felt he wanted to see the event before making a final judgement.

Going back, he spotted a small pond and rode up to water Boss. As he approached the pond, Boss balked and started to whinny. Cal immediately drew his Colt, expecting a miscreant ready to waylay him, or some predator animal ready to attack him. Cal listened and heard some whining noise. Actually, it sounded like some whimpering from a young animal. Cal dismounted and started walking towards the sound. Suddenly, some ten feet from the pond, Cal walked onto a dog. Cal put away his pistol and cautiously approached the dog. He knelt next to it and realized that it was alive. He was breathing but near death. He was a mess. Cal realized that this was probably a dog who had lost a dog fight and was discarded by its owner. The dog was probably trying to get to the pond to drink but likely collapsed before getting there.

Cal took his canteen and added some water to a tin plate. He offered the water and the dog lapped it up. Cal gave him several servings of water and the dog took them aggressively. Cal looked at his injuries. He had several bite marks to the face and one eyelid was nearly closed. He had lost part of one ear and had several bites to his neck and front legs. Many of the bite marks were inflamed, and some had a yellow discharge. It was also apparent that he had been beaten by a human because he had some painful ribs and his right front leg was angled, consisting with a fracture.

Cal said, "well fella, I think you're a fairly young and tough Rottweiler with a bobbed tail, but I don't know if you'll survive. You are covered with blood, look like you have been hit by a train and walked into a pitch fork. With these maximum injuries, if you live, I'll call you Max."

Cal proceeded to set up camp next to the pine trees. He watered his horse and brought him to crop some grass. Boss stepped off the grassy area and walked back to stand over the dog. Cal built a fire and then made a bed of pine branches next to the fire. He then brought his bedroll and folded it into a platform. Carefully, he slid Max to the bedroll and then transferred him to the bed of pine boughs.

Max did not object much. Cal offered him more water till Max finally appeared satisfied and was able to hold up his head.

Cal opened a can of beef stew to heat up while he started to care for Max's wounds. First, he gave Max a bath to clean off the blood and dirt over his fir. He applied carbolic acid to the wounds that appeared inflamed and an antiseptic salve to the others. A splint of two willow branches with a cotton wrap around the leg seemed to stop some painful whimpering.

Meanwhile, Cal noticed that Boss was still watching the goings on. Cal placed some beef stew in a shallow plate and placed it in front of Max. Max lifted his head, looked at the plate and tilted his head sideways to look at Cal. Cal had to smile, the tilted head was saying something that he did not comprehend but thought it could mean, "what's this, you're feeding me?' Cal said, "eat boy, you'll feel better."

Max ate the entire plateful, then gave a soft woof and went to sleep. Cal left a plateful of water next to him and placed a blanket on him. Boss finally walked off to graze. Cal slipped in his bedroll and quickly fell asleep.

In the predawn, Cal woke up to find Max lying next to him, with the blanket still covering him. He had his head up and tilted, as if to say, "I'm hungry." Cal had to smile and got up, went to the bushes and upon his return, Max got up and limped along on Cal's heels. He stirred the coals and rebuilt the fire, added water to boil for coffee and started to cook bacon. Once the water was boiling, he separated it into two pots. One for coffee and the other to cook oatmeal. He added small pieces of bacon, beef jerky, some molasses to the oatmeal and offered it to Max. To Cal's surprise, Max slowly ate the entire batch of "sweet beef and pork oatmeal."

Throughout the morning, Max skipped along on three legs but managed to follow Cal everywhere in camp. It became clear that this dog was intelligent, trainable and would make a good companion. He decided to go to town and buy supplies for at least ten days, including some food for Max. He saddled Boss and said to Max, "stay." To his surprise, Max sat down on his haunches and did not move.

While in town, Cal went to the livery, picked up Buster, and paid the hostler to build a platform that would anchor to the packsaddle. It would fit between the panniers and had sides that would prevent Max from sliding off. At the mercantile, he bought a cowboy scarecrow kit ready to be used after filling it with hay. He also purchased a tent because of the likelihood of rain in the next ten days. He got all the food supplies to last two weeks for him and Max. He also bought a bag of what was called "dry dog food." The storekeeper explained that a Colorado grain plant was experimenting in making food for pets. This was a combination of wheat, oatmeal, dried vegetables especially beets and beef blood. The biggest purchase was beef jerky which provided a high protein satiating diet while on the trail or in cold camps. Other than dry goods, vegetables and meat, he bought fresh eggs, homemade bread and biscuits, which he would enjoy in a long-term camp without traveling.

On his way back to camp, Cal wondered if Max would stay or just take off on his own. The answer was clear as Cal saw Max still sitting in the same spot he had been a few hours ago. After setting down, Boss walked up to Max, bowed his head, and greeted him. Buster followed Boss and gave his own greetings to Max. All three animals smelled each other, and all was well.

Cal joined the mix, squatted down, rubbed Max's head and said, "good dog. Max put his head on his lap and Cal realized this dog was bonding to him. Cal said, "come." Max jumped up and was right on his heels. Cal gave him a couple pieces of jerky while he unloaded the panniers and set up the tent.

Max was curious about this thing. When Cal crawled in and called him to come in, Max slowly stepped in, laid down and tilted his head in apparent wonderment. Cal tried to explain that this was a rain tent, but of course, Max just tilted his head the other way.

The next item on Cal's agenda was the platform. He slowly lifted Max, while talking to him, and placed him on the platform. He said, "lay down boy." Buster started walking next to Cal and they walked several times around the camp. Cal kept peeking at Max and used every bit of energy to avoid laughing. After the experiment, Max was slowly lifted off his "saddle" and returned to the ground. Buster got a carrot and Max got a small piece of jerky. That evening, Max was given a bowl of dry dog food and he crunched it down without hesitation.

The next day, Cal started training Max. The first three commands were sit, stay and come. After he appeared comfortable responding to these commands, Cal added guard, attack and stop. Cal filled the scarecrow with grass and bushes and set it up against a post. Max was a natural, probably because of his dog fighting exposure. He would stand upright on the guard command and stare at the scarecrow. On attack, Max became airborne, knocked the scarecrow down and attached his jaw to the scarecrow's arm that had a pistol attached.

Without the command to stop, Max would tear at the scarecrow's arm in a loud vicious manner.

The next element was following a scent. Cal took one of his old sweaty shirts, bundled it up, had Max smell it and sit. Then Cal dragged the shirt on a string through the grasses, sand, trees, water and any different terrain in the area. When he got to a destination that Max could not see, Cal tore the shirt in half. One half was tied in a tree and the other one was kept, allowing Max to smell it again before the hunt. It took two days and a lot of patience, but Max learned and became proficient in finding his prey.

Cal showed him the meaning of friend by saying the word and rubbing his head and neck behind his ears. At one point, Cal felt that this dog could sense his feelings and emotions. Along this line, Max could communicate with the two horses. He would half bark and or gruff and the horses would nicker back and forth.

At night, Cal would bring Max next to the fire and tell him to guard. Cal wondered if he would ever be capable of warning him of a predator or a human visitor. One late night the horses were grazing far from camp and could not sense a visitor. Max suddenly started growling and pawing at Cals shoulder. Cal heard the scream of a mountain lion. Max jumped in the air and attached himself to the big cat. The fight was furious but eventually, the cat had enough when Max bit him on the nose. The cat took off, but Max got another chunk out of his hind end. Cal looked at Max, who just tilted his head as if to say, "so much for that pussy cat, heh." That night, Cal knew that he had a partner for life.

Over the next week, Cal went riding and Max followed. Max could handle five miles at a slow trot before starting to pant hard. Max would then need water and would allow the free ride on Buster's back for a while. When he was rested, he started jumping off himself but usually asked for help to get onto the platform. After a while, on the command, Max learned to hop on Buster's platform. Cal knew that this would be a sight for unknowing onlookers to behold.

Finally, it started raining one evening. It poured wildly all night and both Cal and Max stayed dry in the tent. That was the night that Cal found out that lightning and thunder bothered Max. He saw Max lay down and place his paws over his ears with his eyes closed. That is when he thought, *this darn dog is smarter than most people!*

After two weeks in camp, the team of two horses, one dog and one bounty hunter headed to town. Cal had a partner that he would learn to trust and rely on, just like his two horses.

***

CHAPTER 2—
The Beginning

The two-mile ride back to Salida was an experience for Max. He rode well and seemed stable on the platform without rolling back and forth. When they arrived in town, people were rubber necking, and some were laughing at the site of Max riding on Buster's back.

Arriving at the livery, the attendant was an older gent by the name of Zeke, who looked at Max and said, "Mister, that's the funniest site I've ever seen. When you were here ten days ago, I thought the platform you wanted was to haul more goods, not a dog. Now tell me why you're giving him a ride?"

"I'm a bounty hunter and I can travel up to forty miles a day. I need this dog as a partner and can't afford to exhaust him by walking all that distance. He can walk as much as he wants, but when I see he's getting tired, I'll tell him to jump up, and he'll ride for a while."

"Now will you take care of my horses for a few days and can I leave Max here. All you need to do is keep water in his dish and give him half a bowl of this dog food twice a day." "Sure." "In that case, Max this is a 'friend,' now rub his head and give him this piece of jerky. From now on he'll respond to sit, stay, guard, speak, attack and several other commands. If he doesn't understand the command, he'll tilt his head. Just change the command till he responds. He is friendly, but if you are threatened, he will defend you. Anytime he does something that pleases you, give him a small piece of beef jerky."

Cal took his saddlebags and walked over to the local hotel situated in the center of town. He rented a room, and went to the tonsorial shop for a shave, haircut and a hot bath. After he bathed, he gave his clothes to be laundered. He then changed into his second set of clothes, went to the saloon for a few beers, and a game of poker.

Cal had decided to stay in town for a week. He predicted that the Spencer gang would be back to rob the bank to get the payroll they could not get when they robbed the train two weeks ago. He then sent a telegram to the sheriffs of bordering towns, requesting that they notify him if the gang showed up in their community. Cal then settled down to await some news of the Spencer gang's activity.

Cal spent his days playing poker. One day he had a friendly game going when a well-dressed gent showed up and joined their table. He introduced himself as the bank president, Horace Green. The conversation turned to Cal and Mr. Green asked what Cal did for a living. "I'm a bounty hunter and I'm waiting for the Spencer gang." "Do you think they'll be back?" "Yes, I think they will come back to rob your bank. If I was you, I would add a deputy sheriff as security in your bank during work hours for a few weeks." "I think that's a good idea and will arrange this with Sheriff Williams."

A few days later, Cal went to the livery to see how Zeke was doing with Max. Zeke said, "I like your dog. He is a pleasure to have around. Every time he tilts his head, I start laughing. One day, I had two smart-ass hard men, sons of a rich rancher, who tried to stiff me for taking care of their horses. I said to Max, guard and speak. Max came up to me and started growling. When he showed them his teeth, they both shelled out full payment and quickly left. Max got a full beef jerky as my thanks. I'm so pleased with him that I decided to get myself a rottweiler puppy and train him as a guard dog."

That evening, Cal was having dinner at the local diner when he heard gunshots. He paid for his meal and stepped outside. People were running to the bank. When he got there, the sheriff was already organizing a posse. He said that the robbers were the Spencer gang and the railroad had a $10,000 reward on them. Within minutes, he had a posse of fifteen men ready to ride for the reward. President Green also said that he would add a reward of $1,000 for the return of the $6,000 that was stolen.

After the posse departed, Cal talked to President Green. "Was anyone killed or wounded?" "Yes, the deputy was shot in the thigh and is in bad shape at Doc Emerson's office. Unfortunately, my head teller was killed when he could not open the vault since he didn't have the combination. I opened it and they emptied all our cash plus the payroll for several mines. If we don't recover the money, we will have to close our doors."

Cal could hear a woman and children crying. He stepped into the bank and saw a woman with three kids kneeling over the dead bank clerk. Cal had an epiphany. *As he watched the grieving family, he suddenly became conscious of something that was important to him. He knew he had just had an illumination. He had found the meaning and purpose for his bounty hunting profession—justice for the victims.*

Cal stepped back and asked President Green, "what happens to this man's family?" "Mr. Wick was making $50 a month. My parent company will compensate his wife $1,000. Mrs. Wick works as a home seamstress but may need to work nights as a waitress to support her family. They still owe $1000 on their house mortgage, so times will be hard for her."

Cal walked away from the morbid scene and headed to the livery. "Zeke let's settle my account and would you saddle my horses. I'm going after the Spencer gang." He then went to the mercantile and bought another change of clothes, a winter coat, woolen socks and food for a week on the road. After getting Boss, Buster and Max, he loaded his supplies and rode out south of town. Max was walking next to Buster.

***

After riding for a few miles, Cal met the sheriff and his posse. They looked beat up and discouraged as they trailed 5 bodies draped over the horses' saddles. Cal looked at the sheriff and asked, "what happened?" "The gang was waiting to ambush us. We walked right into a massive shootout. We lost five good men and were lucky to escape with our lives. These five outlaws are murderers and very dangerous gunfighters. It's going to take an army to bring them down." "Tell President Green that I'll bring back his money and the railroad's gold."

Cal stayed on the road and suddenly came

to a location that was suspicious. Cal had a premonition that this area would be ideal for an ambush. He pulled his sawed-off shotgun loaded with 00 buckshot and slowly advanced. He knew that if the outlaws were there waiting for him, he would fire both barrels at them. This would give him time to find some protection or retreat. As he advanced, he saw large pools of dried blood and realized that this was where the posse was ambushed.

Cal continued riding and when darkness came, he found a spot next to a stream with good grass and decent cover. He unsaddled the horses, brought them to water and set them in the grassy areas without a tether, hobble or ground hitch. They would not walk away from camp. Cal dug a firepit and started a small fire to cook dinner. He fried some thin slices of potatoes with onions and then added them to a can of beef stew. Max was laying next to his bowl waiting for some food. Cal had his dinner and the leftovers were added to Max's bowl.

After dinner, Cal was thinking of Mrs. Wick and reliving that sad scene. He knew that this lady and her kids needed justice. The $1,000 compensation would not be enough to support this family. She could continue being a seamstress but an evening job as a waitress would not be conducive to maintain a family life. With one child in school and two still at home, she needed to be home with them.

Cal thought that Mrs. Wick and similar victims needed assistance to overcome the bad hand they had been given. First, they needed legal justice which involved capturing the outlaws that caused the depredations. Secondly, they needed security and protection from those that would threaten the victims. And last, they needed adequate financial compensation and the means to support themselves.

Cal decided that by capturing the outlaws, he could use the monetary bounties to provide short and long-term security, financial support and whatever else they needed. This would be his mission—to provide victims' justice.

He then laid out his plans to capture the Spencer gang. He thought, *this five-member gunfighter gang will be dangerous to apprehend.*

They will likely bypass the small towns on the way and head to Alamosa. I suspect they have a camp outside of Alamosa where they've been hiding since the train gold heist. I can only hope that they use Alamosa for their entertainment. If that's the case, I will try to apprehend them while in town or follow them to their camp for the final confrontation.

Meanwhile in the Spencer camp, the gang leader is saying, "we shot up the posse enough that they quit and went back home. Whether we have a bounty hunter on our tail will not matter. We are ahead and will continue traveling forty to fifty miles tomorrow and be at camp the next day. We are dividing the $6,000 in five parts, so keep the bulk in your money belt so you don't flash large bundles of greenbacks. We will continue going into town in groups of two, to avoid the appearance of a gang and avoid suspicion."

The next day, traveling was uneventful. Cal stopped every two hours to water the horses. Lunch lasted a half hour and allowed the horses to feed on oats and do some grazing. Max had been following Buster all day, but when it was time to get back on the road, he automatically jumped up on Buster for a free ride.

The next day Cal arrived in Alamosa by 4PM. He brought his horses and Max to the livery. Left his gear at the livery except for his saddlebags and his shotgun. Went to the railroad hotel and took a room with a hot bath. He then headed to the sheriff's office.

The deputy introduced him to Sheriff Macon. "What can I do for you?" "My name is Cal Harnell. I sent you a telegram two weeks ago asking if you had seen the Spencer gang?" "Yeah, I got it. I can tell you that my deputy and I are not gunfighters, and if the gang was here, I wouldn't engage them. However, we have not seen any gangs and we don't go looking in the six saloons to match reward posters against any of the patrons."

"I understand, can I see the dodgers of all five members?" "Sure can." Cal went through the posters and found all five members. The sheriff gave him a copy of each one. Cal thanked him and said, "I expect this gang is camped nearby and will come into town for their entertainment. I will be apprehending them and will try to avoid a shootout."

He then went to Rosa's diner and ordered the special of the day, chicken and dumplings with fresh bread, peas, coffee and bread pudding for dessert.

Waiting for his meal, he reviewed the posters and committed them to memory. He had a great tasting dinner and left a dollar for a 50-cent meal and tip.

After dinner he decided to visit the six saloons. Before starting he went to his room and changed into less conspicuous clothing. He went from all black to some dirty clothes, a bright blue shirt, canvas beige pants and an old deformed grey felt hat. With an old beat up holster to hold his Colt and his burlap bag to carry his sawed-off shotgun and manacles, he looked like a homesteader that came to town on foot to get supplies.

After getting Max, he left him sitting on the boardwalk and entered the first saloon. There was one table of card players and the men were not on the wanted posters. The second saloon had a few cowboys standing at the bar, also not on the posters. The third saloon, "The ten of diamonds," was packed with patrons. Leaving Max outside, he stepped to the bar and ordered a nickel beer. He stood at the bar and looked over at the many patrons and saloon gals. In the far-right corner were two men that were on the reward posters.

Cal grabbed his sawed-off shotgun, walked right up to the table, and pointed his shotgun at the two outlaws. Loud and clear, he said, "put your hands up, I know you are members of the Spencer gang, and I'm bringing you to jail." The outlaws had no choice, with a shotgun in their faces, they stood and put their hands up.

Cal calls, "Max come, guard, and speak." Max starts growling, shows his teeth, and had his hackles up. "Bartender put your hands on the bar and the rest you, clear out of here— NOW." After the room was cleared, the bartender was ordered to close the overnight doors that covered the batwing doors and to close the two windows' inside shutters. "Now put your hands behind your back, and bartender, take the manacles out of my burlap bag and place them on these miscreants."

With the outlaws in control, the doors were opened, and they stepped outside to be greeted by Sheriff Macon. "Well Mr. Harnell, I'm glad to see it's you and that you don't need any help." "No, but I would appreciate the use of your jail." "Be glad to help. Follow me and you folks can go back in the saloon."

Arriving at the sheriff's office, Cal said, "these are murderers and under no circumstance do you or your deputy open this jail door. Let them use the bucket chamber pot for nature's call and don't open the door to empty the pot unless they are manacled to the bars. Slide their meals under the bars. I will pay each of you $5 a night to sleep in the jail and I will be back with the other three as soon as possible. Do not, I repeat, do not let them out of the cell under any circumstance. If you do, someone will die. If you're not comfortable housing them, hire extra guns and I will also pay them $5 a day." The last thing Cal did was search the prisoner's pockets and found $2,400 which he left in the sheriff's safe but pocketed the $89 of extra cash.

The next day no one was seen who matched the wanted posters. Cal knew that someone would show up looking for their partners.

Meanwhile at the Spencer camp, "something is wrong. Slim and Stan were supposed to be back last night. Winston, I want you to go to town and check all the saloons, especially the 'Palace' which has overnight rooms and meals."

That same late afternoon, a lone rider came in and tied his horse at the first of six saloons. The man would walk in a saloon and be out within five minutes. He was obviously looking for someone.

By the time he entered the fourth saloon, the Palace, Cal had an idea. He stepped up to the outlaw's horse and quickly took out an old shirt out of the saddlebags. He rubbed it on the horse, had Max smell it, and then pocketed it. He rushed to the livery and had Boss saddled. He then went back to the hotel's porch and watched the outlaw hit the last two saloons. He was last seen talking with some town bystanders who were seen pointing at the sheriff's office, then got on his horse and left town.

Cal waited a half hour and then headed north. He stopped, had Max smell the tainted shirt and told Max to "find." Max took off with his nose to the ground. An hour later, Max smelled something that Cal did not appreciate. He stopped, sat on his haunches and gave a soft muffled bark. Cal tied Boss to a tree, grabbed his shotgun with extra shells and followed Max till he could see and smell camp fire smoke. He then took the lead and snuck up to camp till he could hear them talk.

"So, they weren't in any saloon and someone told you they were in jail. We have just lost $2,400 and have been found. So, it's time to get out of here. Call Jackson back from the river where he is bathing and let's close camp." "Where are we going?" "We're heading east to Walsenburg some 80 miles from here."

Cal crept up to within fifteen yards and saw two men talking. He called out, "put your hands up, I've got you covered with a shotgun." Winston never hesitated, he drew his Colt. Cal had anticipated that one or both would draw on him and he pulled the trigger on one barrel. The bulk of the buckshot load smacked Winston's left shoulder and twisted him around before he fell to the ground. The other outlaw screamed out. A few pellets hit him in his right arm and hand, and his pistol fell to the ground.

While the outlaws were still in shock, Cal placed their arms around a tree and manacled their wrists. He then said, "where is your other buddy?" "There was only Winston and me." "Bull-ticky, I just heard you mention that Jackson was bathing and why do you have three bedrolls laid out?" "Go to Hell!"

Cal looks at Max and says, "Max, find and attack." A few minutes later, a horrifying scream and hollering was heard in the bushes. Cal ran to the site and saw Max laying over a nude outlaw with a good mouthful hold on his shooting arm. Cal picked up his pistol, called Max off, got him to dress before he walked him back to camp and manacled him to a tree.

Cal then checked the outlaw's pockets and gathered all $3,600 and some $119 in small cash. The petty cash went into his pocket and the $3,600 went in his saddlebags. Cal tells Max to guard while he goes back to get Boss. Max steps up to the outlaws, growls and bares his teeth, and the outlaws immediately turned behind the tree just to get away.

When Cal returned with Boss, he took the neck shackles out. He attached the neck collar and secured the chain to the tree. He then changed the manacles to move their arms behind their backs. He tied the pistols and rifles in the outlaw pack horse's panniers. He loaded the gold bars in several saddle-bags and distributed them on the horses. Finally, with the outlaws mounted, their neck collar chains locked to a stirrup, the caravan headed to Alamosa.

An hour later, the five-horse caravan arrived at the sheriff's office. Sheriff Macon said, "well Cal, you have sand. You did what was necessary to capture this dangerous bunch of murderers. You have my respect." After the outlaws were placed in their cells, Cal went to the railroad office to secure passage to Salida. He pre-arranged to board the four outlaws in the stock car where their neck shackles could be locked to a wall mounted ring.

The next day Cal had the local doc come to the jail to remove the buckshot pellets from the outlaw's bodies. He didn't want them to die of an infection before they could hang. Afterwards, he went to a local gun shop and sold the five pistols for $125 and the five 1873 rifles for $200. He also bought a Webley Bulldog. The local livery bought the five horses with saddles and tack for $280. The railroad reward, bounty on their heads, and the bank reward would be collected once they arrived in Salida.

That afternoon, Cal notified Sheriff Williams that he would be arriving with the Spencer gang by 4PM and requested some assistance in transferring the outlaws to jail and picking up the gold. Later, Cal boarded a stock car with Boss Buster, Mac, four outlaws and a fortune in gold. The train arrived on time and the sheriff/deputies, railroad detectives, and President Green were there to greet them.

Over the next several days, the sheriff was able to get the bounty rewards sent by telegraph voucher. The bounties amounted to $1,000 per outlaw. The railroad reward was $10,000, the sale of the guns and horses at $600, and with the bank reward, it all added to $16,600.

Cal placed $600 in his money belt, deposited $12,000 in the bank, and arranged for a bank transfer to his account in the Denver National Bank. He opened an account in Green's Bank and deposited the other $4,000 and accepted several bank drafts. President Green was a bit surprised when the account was opened in Lorie Ann Wick's name. He then added to the deposit, the $1,000 life insurance that the parent company was awarding her.

The last thing on Cal's agenda was meeting with Mrs. Wick. Cal came to her house and knocked. The lady opened the door and asked if he had some sewing jobs for her. Cal said, "no Ma'am. I am the bounty hunter who just captured your husband's murderers— the Spencer gang. May I speak with you?" "Certainly, please come in."

Mrs. Wick asked if they were brought in dead or alive. "Yes Ma'am, they are all alive and they will likely hang after their trial." "Thank you for providing some justice on behalf of my husband." Cal then asked, "not to be blunt, but I am willing to give you some financial assistance. How do you plan to support yourself with three kids?" "I still have four years to pay off the house mortgage at $20 a month. I will continue to do some sewing alterations and will likely need to look for a waitress job, to make ends meet."

"Ma'am, you need to be home with your kids in the evenings. Please accept this bank deposit." Mrs. Wick looks at the amount and says, "I cannot accept this." "Yes, you can. It includes $1,000 as the life insurance the bank is giving you, and $4,000 from me. These funds come from my 'victim benefactor fund.'" Mrs. Wick starts crying.

"In addition to the money, you need security and protection. I see you have a shotgun by the door. Do you know how to use it?" "Yes, and I have my husband's Smith and Wesson pistol which I know how to shoot." "Please add this pistol, a Webley Bulldog that will fit in your pocket or reticule."

"Being a widow, you will have male visitors

requesting sexual favors for money. Greet them at the door with a shotgun and they'll likely never return. In addition, if ever you need my assistance because you're physically threatened, send a telegram to Amos Farley in Silver Circle, and he will find me. I will return to assist you, that's a promise." Mrs. Wicks was still crying.

"How do I thank you." "By paying off your mortgage, continue doing some sewing, raise your kids and enjoy life. You'll likely be lucky and find a good man to marry you and love your kids. If this doesn't happen, you have the means to remain independent." "Thank you and be safe."

Cal prepared to leave town and Sheriff Macon said, "the trial is in three days, and how do I reach you if your testimony is needed?" "Send a telegram to Amos Farley in Silver Circle and I will return."

Cal took the train to Silver Circle and had no idea how this visit would change the direction of his life.

***

CHAPTER 3—Sponsorship

When Cal arrived in Silver Circle, he brought his two horses to the nearest livery, Hawkins Livery. The hostler introduced himself and said, "my name is Bruce Hawkins, how may I help you." "Would you care for my horses and dog? I am visiting a friend at the W—M Connected Ranch for a few days." Bruce agreed, and Cal gave the usual line about Max's care and food. With Bruce's directions, Cal mounted Boss and headed to the ranch for a visit with Amos.

Arriving at the ranch, Cal's horse was stopped on a knoll where he could see the center of the ranch. The view was of a small village. The buildings included three separate homes with outbuildings and a large bunkhouse/cook shack. The barn was extra large for many horses and there were three other massive structures, an implement shed and two haybale's storage sheds. The center of activity was the location of four "one horse balers" with several men to keep it operational, and a long conveyor belt transferring haybales to a railroad box car.

Cal rode up and tied Boss's reins to the hitchrail. He stepped up to the baling platform. He was amazed at what he saw. A horse was walking in a circle on his own to turn a cam which activated the cutting plunger. Two men were feeding the baler, two men were attaching strings to the bales and one man was bringing the bales to the conveyor. A few men were receiving the bales and stacking them in the boxcar. Wagons were continually arriving from the fields with more hay that was being unloaded next to the balers. The unloading process included a hoisting system of a hay hook implanted in the load of loose hay. The hay was lifted off the wagon by horse power and dropped on the pile next to each baler.

Cal was watching the entire process of unloading each wagon and baling the hay. He noticed that the last baler had two older ladies who were frantically working to keep the baler fed. Cal stepped up, took a hay fork and started to help the ladies. One lady said, "well hello sir, what brings you to the W—M Ranch?" "Visiting one of your employees, Amos Farley. My name is Cal Harnell. You look like you could use some assistance and I'm glad to help."

"Yes, this is crunch time and when the fourth baler is needed to keep up production, we often run short of help. That is why we are helping. I am Cora Swanson and my buddy is Sally Winslow, mother and mother-in-law." They worked together till the next water break. Sally then mentioned that Amos was running the dump rake and would not be back till the hay was all picked up or darkness arrived. Cal answered, "well then, I guess you get free help for the rest of the day, heh."

Work restarted, and Cal went back to work. He could not help but notice a man giving orders and asked, "is that your son?" "No, that's Henry McDuff, the farm foreman. He is here, there and everywhere. He will often relieve a worker that is showing fatigue, just to keep the system going. My son is the twine man on baler #3. He is also the owner and general manager of the cattle ranch and the crop farm. And yes, like Henry, he also works on the line when needed."

During lunch, two baler teams went to the cook shack. Teams #1 and 2 were first and teams #3 and 4 were last. Wayne Swanson came up to Cal while eating their lunch. "Are you looking for work?" "No, I'm a bounty hunter and stopped here to visit with my old partner, Amos Farley. When he retired, he wanted me to work with a sponsor, and thought that I should talk with you about it." "Be glad to sit down with you after the crunch time is over, but that may be a few days." "Not a problem, for room and board I will continue working on the baling platform till we can talk." "Wow, what a deal for me." He then introduced Cal to Henry with an explanation of his work status. He also had the hostler take care of his horse. Before returning to work, Cal brought his rifles and saddlebags to the bunkhouse and chose one of the free bunks.

During the next three days, Cal continued to feed hay in the balers. He visited with Amos during the evenings. Amos said, "I love the work, the food is great, and the people are friendly. I plan to continue working half days as soon as the crunch is over. I'm in the process of buying a small house with barn in town and enjoy being with my brother and his large family. Plus, my brother has a year-round job on the farm and we are both well paid."

Three days later, as promised, Wayne sat down and had a long talk with Cal. Cal told his story of the year spent with Amos, bringing the Spencer gang to justice, his recent decision to financially support the victims of violent crimes, and the suggestion that a sponsor would be the best way to operate a bounty hunting service on a mission.

Wayne was very attentive. "What are your talents and methods?" "I'm highly proficient at fast draw and tracking. I have a dog as a partner. I bring half of the outlaws back alive. I don't shoot outlaws in the back. Most important, I use the monetary rewards to compensate the victims and help them find a way to support themselves."

Wayne finally said, "I'm impressed, and Amos has strongly recommended you for this job. Captain Ennis of the US Marshall Service has been looking for my replacement. I was a bounty hunter sponsored by Captain Ennis. Six months ago, he asked me to recommend an experienced bounty hunter to act on their behalf. I think you are that person, and if you accept I will give you a letter of reference to give to Capt. Ennis in Denver."

"Yes sir, I'm interested. Do you have any recommendations?" "Yes, get a backpack holster for a sawed-off shotgun. Buy some of these new 50X telescopic binoculars with leather hoods and a tripod to stabilize it. Carry moccasins for walking quietly, and in the winter, use some horse blankets for nighttime when the temperature is below zero."

"I am giving you this awl." "What is it for, I'm not a carpenter?" "When you want to know something from a captive, there is no need for physical torture, which often fails. Just open their mouths and stick the pointed end in a rotten tooth. Giggle it around and you'll see the results in the outlaw's face and in his hollering. Generally, you won't need a second application."

"Well thank you." "I'll be heading to Denver tomorrow by train." "That's fine, my father-in-law is going to town for parts and I'll have him send a telegram to Capt. Ennis informing him of your arrival. Good luck and stay safe, the victims need you."

***

Cal left his two horses with Bruce Hawkins and took the train east to Pueblo. There he changed trains and headed north directly to Denver. Arriving in the city, he took a buggy taxi to the Marshall Headquarters. As he entered the captain's office, he introduced himself to the receiving deputy. The deputy said, "yes sir, we have been expecting you, please follow me to the captain's office."

"Welcome Mr. Harnell. Wayne has given you a strong recommendation and I am glad to see you." "Please call me Cal." "To maintain office decorum, please call me Captain. Let's start talking about your mission of 'victim's justice."' Cal proudly explained his goals toward assisting victims and the topics moved on.

"Vert good, your mission is similar to the crusade Wayne Swanson followed. Let's move on. I will explain the Marshal Service and what we would like from you. We serve processes and hunt criminals as ordered by government courts and judges. Our income is from fees for serving processes and bounties on criminals."

"What are government processes?" "We serve subpoenas, writs of habeous corpus, writs of mandamus, file charges of malfeasance, and warrants. We also provide protection for federal judges, transfer prisoners, stop range wars, and settle mining disputes."

"Regarding criminals on the run, how do you choose which ones to hunt?" "We respond to orders sent by federal and district judges, and requests for help by city marshals and sheriffs. But because of our limited number of deputies and their training, we don't undertake gunfighting violent criminals when a gunfight is expected. Also, we limit our jurisdiction to major cities from Cheyenne to Trinidad along the north/south main railroad."

"So, you need help capturing violent criminals and assisting distant communities such as Durango, Montrose, Grand Junction, and the Eastern Ranches all the way to the Oklahoma Indian Nations!"

"Yes sir, plus we expect a certain level of respectful behavior. You are not an executioner. You are a representative of US law. To achieve your goals safely, you can use whatever method is necessary to apprehend, dead or alive, and or resolve a situation. In short, the reputation you earn will be the result of your activity—a choice you have to make."

"This is a very dangerous job and if you accept the position, I will swear you in and give you this badge. You will not be on the payroll and your pay will be the reward bounties. In addition, you can claim their horses, guns, pocket cash, and saddlebags' contents."

Cal looked at the badge which read, "Deputy US Marshall—Special Duty," After a minute in deep thought, Cal said, "Captain,

I appreciate the offer and I'm proud to accept. I won't let you down." The official witnessed swearing-in took place and the badge was applied to his vest. Cal thanked him and said, "what is my first assignment, Captain?

"Durango, this is a large town of over a thousand people that has grown to support the mining and timber industries. It has smelters that process the retrieval of metals from ores brought in by train or freight wagons. It became the smelting center because of its good supply of water and coal needed to support the extraction process."

"The smelter's product is bars of gold, silver and other precious metals. These are stored in the Central Bank's vault. The bouillon is then transferred to another financial center in Pueblo where it is converted to paper currency and a portion is sent back to Durango's Central Bank by bullet proof cars with a vault and several railroad detectives. From there the payroll is distributed to the many mines around Durango. This is where you come in."

"The payroll cash distribution is the

problem. Robberies are common place and the security personnel have been devastated. The have tried sending cash by stagecoach, wagons and single horses with large security details. No matter the method, they are robbed, and everyone killed."

"It appears that there are two groups involved. Someone is leaking information of the cash shipments to the outlaws. We know who the spies are, and we could go ahead and round them up. But, we don't know the master organizer and we know he can be identified by the outlaws. We feel the outlaws have to be captured first."

"How many outlaws are we dealing with?" "Three gangs of four to five members. They live in saloons that provide food, lodging, saloon gals and liquor. The Murdock gang is in the Silver King, the Greeley gang is in Craig's Place, and the Benson gang is in the Ace of Clubs. These are gunfighters and killers. No lawman will go up against them because they know it's suicide. All these outlaws have a price on their heads and the master organizer has a

$2,000 reward. When you get to town, stop and see the city marshal, Marshal Lockwood."

"Ok, I'm going back to Silver Circle to pick up my horses, gear and guns. I will then head out to Durango by train." Captain Ennis added, "it's 150 miles from Denver to Silver Circle. By train, at an average of 30 mph, that's approximately five hours or at least four days by horse. It's also 300 miles from Silver Circle to Durango. That's also 10 hours by train or nine days by horse." "Wow, I can certainly handle fifteen hours on a train compared to some thirteen days on a horse."

"Well, let's hope for a good outcome, don't take extreme chances, and stay safe. I expect you back here after completing this assignment. During that meeting, we'll discuss your next job."

***

Cal arrived in Silver Circle after a long nap. As he stepped onto the platform, he spotted a telegraph messenger holding a card that said, "Cal Harnell." Cal stepped up to the messenger who said, "this gram arrived two hours ago for Mr. Amos Farley. Since it was marked urgent, I delivered it to Mr. Farley and after reading it, he paid me to wait for you here and deliver it to you." "Thanks, and here's four bits for your trouble." "Thanks sir." Cal read the telegram.

TO AMOS FARLEY, SILVER CIRCLE CO -STOP- HAVE BEEN ASSAULTED AND FEAR FOR MY LIFE -STOP- NEED ASSISTANCE -STOP- PLEASE NOTIFY CAL HARNELL -STOP FROM LORIE WICK, SALIDA CO.

Cal turned around and said to the conductor, "sir, I will be continuing to Salida. How long before the train departs?" "We're only taking on water and coal, we'll be resuming our trip in fifteen minutes." Cal paid the fee and landed in Salida an hour later. After stepping on the platform, he walked directly to the Wick's home. After knocking, he heard a slow shuffle and the door was slowly opened. In front of Cal stood Mrs. Wick who was holding a shotgun but looked a mess. She had black and blue bruises to her left face and a coon's shiner on her left eye. She was walking bent over and had a cast on her left hand. She then placed the shotgun down and started crying. Cal stepped up, encircled her in a hug and said, "I'll take care of this, and it'll never happen again!"

"Now, tell me what happened." "Three hours ago, a local man, by the name of Reese Stokes, knocked at the door, and requested sexual favors. He offered me $2, and I may have been rude to him when I told him that I did not perform such activities. When I went to pick up my shotgun, he pushed the screen door in my face, punched me in the face, knocked me down, kicked me in the ribs and back, stepped on my hand and broke several bones. Fortunately, after the beating, he left, while saying he would be back and expected a more pleasant greeting followed by a wild evening. Thank goodness he didn't rape me in front of my kids. My six-year-old son went to get Sheriff Williams who brought my kids to our neighbor and brought me to see Doc Moore. While I was at the Doc's office, Sheriff Williams sent the telegram that I prepared. That was just a few hours ago, how did you get here so fast?"

"The telegraph messenger met me at the railroad platform and handed me the telegram you sent to Amos Farley. I reembarked the train and here I am. Do you think this man will show up again tonight?" "Yes, he's such a crass individual that he'll likely show up when it's dark. My kids will be staying the night at the neighbor, and I was planning to receive him with my shotgun." "Well, I'll be here to greet him, heh!"

"Ok, then let me prepare some dinner for you. During the meal, Cal asked her if she had used some of the funds. "I used $1,000 to pay off the mortgage and used $200 to buy clothes and shoes for everyone, as well as food for the pantry and sewing supplies. I have $100 in cash for the near future and the rest of the money is in the bank." "Great."

After dinner they waited in the main room and shortly later, someone knocked at the door. Mrs. Wick opened the screen door and said, "well Mr. Stokes, I was expecting you." The man was smiling and stepped through the door. Suddenly, Cal grabbed him by his vest and threw him in mid air to land against the wall. He was stunned and went for his gun. Cal grabbed his gun hand and violently pushed his trigger and mid finger a full 180 degrees backwards. Stokes screamed a blood curdling noise and Cal then twisted both fingers till the bones broke. He then pummeled his face with two round house punches, dragged him to the porch and threw him to the ground.

Cal stepped off the porch and fired his pistol at the sky. People were arriving to see what was happening, including Sheriff Williams and his deputies. Cal proceeded to lift Stokes shoulders off the ground and turned his face to a bloody pulp with one punch after another till he lost consciousness. Cal yells out, "This pea brain came to Mrs. Wick demanding sexual favors and beat her in front of her kids. Pass the word around, any man coming to her home with such demands will be treated the same way. I promise, no matter where I am in this state, when I get a telegram of such activity, I will return and give any man the same treatment. Mrs. Wick is a seamstress with a family, not a whore."

Sheriff Williams asked, "Mrs. Wick, are you pressing charges?" "Yes." "Good, bring this piece of crap to jail and have Doc Moore fix his hand and check him out. The Judge will likely sentence him to a month's jail time for aggravated assault." As the crowd cleared, Sheriff Williams said to Cal, "I now understand your mission. You promised victims' justice—assistance and protection. I wish I could have done the same when this happened, but the law does not allow a lawman to administer due punishment. I didn't stop you when you were beating him because you were dishing out the correct justice—but you never heard it from me."

Feeling the issue was resolved, Cal returned to Silver Circle to get his horses, guns, supplies and Max. He then took the train and adjusted to a ten-hour ride to Durango.

***

On arrival, he brought his horses and gear to the livery located next to the saloons, hotel and marshal's office. The hotel, the Durango Plaza, was a mid-range enterprise with facilities for a hot bath, public water closets and coffee twenty hours a day. Meals were available at the nearby diner, Marie's Place.

After settling in and having a nice cold roast beef sandwich and coffee at Marie's Place, Cal went to the marshal's office. As he entered, he introduced himself to the three deputies and asked to see the marshal. Entering the marshal's office, Cal said, "hello sir, I'm US Deputy Marshal Harnell sent here by Captain Ennis to assist you." "Nice to get the help. My name is Marshal Lockwood. Where are your deputies?" "Please call me Cal and I'm alone with my dog." "Well son, I asked for a team of at least four marshals. It's suicide to go against a dozen gunfighter outlaws." "Not a problem, I can handle them and will bring all into custody, dead or alive." "Ok, but it's your funeral."

"Tell me when you lost your last shipment." "It was a week ago, the stagecoach with two men riding shotgun and two guards in the coach was devastated when outlaws dropped a tree on the coach as it passed by. The driver and three armed guards were killed instantly and the fourth died a day later after he verified that the Murdock gang were the culprits that stole the payroll cash worth $10,000." "With the proof you have, why haven't you arrested them?" "Because it's suicidal for me and my three deputies to go up against these gunfighters—we didn't sign up for that." "Well I did, so keep the jail cells available, I'll be back with some prisoners."

Cal stepped outside, picked up Max and headed for the Silver King saloon. On entering with Max, the bartender told Cal to take his dog outside. Cal drew his sawed-off shotgun out of his backpack holster and said, "tell me who the Murdock gang is and keep your hands on the bar." "First table on the right and you won't get any trouble from me."

Cal moves over, puts his back to the wall and says, "Murdock and your toadies, stand and put your hands up." The four men turned and when they saw the shotgun, complied by standing and facing Cal. "I said put your hands up." No one was following his orders and Murdock then went for his gun. Cal yells, "attack". Max jumped and grabbed Murdock's crotch. Murdock folded over and collapsed to the floor. "You three, up with the hands or get a mouthful from Max." The hands went up as all three tried to move away from Max's drooling mouth.

Cal looked at the patrons and said, "which one of you is not wearing a gun and wants to earn $5." One hand goes up. "Fine, step up and the rest of you clear the room till I secure these outlaws." Once clear, "first, pick up their four pistols and place them on the bar. Now you three turn around with your hands in your back so this gent can place manacles on you. Also put manacles on Murdock and then throw a glass of beer in his face to wake him up."

As Cal and the Murdock gang were stepping out of the saloon, they were met by Marshal Lockwood. "Thanks for coming to the party, would you take their guns to your office and these three to your jail while I have a talk with the great Mr. Murdock." "Certainly, see you later."

Cal pushed Murdock back in the saloon and said, "get on the floor on your back." "Why, so you can torture me?" "If you don't get down, I'll put you down with a lot of hurt!" "I don't think so, since lawmen don't torture." Without hesitation, Cal steps aside, draws his pistol, and shoots Murdock's knee cap to smithereens. Murdock fell to the floor screaming expletives and threatening to kill Cal.

With Murdock on his back, Cal straddles him on his chest and says, "you are going to tell me who the master organizer of this caper is. You made the decision to die an hour ago when you drew on me, but it so happens that Max robbed you of a quick death. Now you will hang. It seems to me that you owe this bit of relief and revenge to the dead men's families." "Go to hell lawman."

Without another word, Cal pulls out his awl from his back pocket and forces Murdock's mouth open. Cal then chooses a rotten molar and shoves the awl's pointed end deep in the tooth's nerve root. There were a couple seconds of silence then the end of the world was in Murdock's eyes. Murdock went still, then his eyes bulged out of his head, followed by his pupils dilating. Then came the screaming and hollering from hell as he wet himself and his bowels emptied. The screaming changed to a high pitch squeal as Cal was moving the awl in all directions.

Finally, Cal pulled the awl and asked him again who the lead man was. "Who is conveying the spies info, informing the outlaws, and paying everyone off per robbery?" Murdock shook his head in the negative. Cal forced his mouth and shoved the awl in another tooth. Instead of Murdock screaming, he was trying to say "loooowhur." Cal pulled the awl and Murdock said, "it's a lawyer on Main Street by the name of Wilhelm Hocksler."

Upon returning to the sheriff's office the deputies took Murdock to a water basin and stripped him down. He was scrubbed with stiff brush, rinsed off and changed into clean pants. Cal mentioned the knee cap area needed bandaging. Sheriff Lockwood said, "not necessary, Judge Stanley has set the trial for this afternoon at 5PM. We have several witnesses against them and they'll likely hang at dawn."

"Now tell me, the gunshot was followed by Murdock swearing and threatening to kill you. What on earth did you do to cause that man to squeal like a tortured hog—there were no marks on him." "Well Sheriff, I was as surprised as you were. It was the first time I used this tool. It's an awl with a fine point and you just shove it into the center of a bad tooth cavity and watch the result." "Oh my, I felt that in my head. That probably accounts why he's still puckering his lips, heh."

The trial ended with a unanimous guilty verdict. Judge Stanley sentenced them to hang at dawn tomorrow. After the prisoners were returned to their cells, Sheriff Lockwood expressed concern that the Greeley and or the Benson gang might try to break them out before morning. Cal suggested, "Sheriff, you and your deputies arm yourselves with shotguns, barricade the doors, and post a deputy in each window. Max and I will walk the outside perimeter of the jail all night and try to ward off an attack. We should be Ok till morning."

At 3AM, Max started growling and Cal finally heard someone talking. Cal heard, "you two guys carry this log and ram it into the jail's back door. Sam and I will be your back up and we'll shoot the jailer."

Cal quickly moved behind the privy and waited. When the log carriers arrived and were about to ram the door, Cal shot both carriers with his sawed-off shotgun. The other two outlaws retreated when they saw the result caused by a mad man shooting a double barrel shotgun.

The massive shotgun blasts awoke the neighbors who were coming out to see what was going on. Sheriff Lockwood came outside, looked at the log and two dead outlaws, and said, "I don't think their buddies will be back tonight. Thanks for the help, again!"

When dawn arrived, spectators were already waiting at the gallows. All four outlaws were walked up the gallows, hung two at a time, by using the double trap doors. After the total of six dead outlaws were picked up by the undertaker, Sheriff Lockwood invited Cal to his office. "You have some major money coming. Here is the current value: The four horses and tact were sold for $300. The six Colt pistols and four 1873 rifles sold for another $300. All six outlaws had pocket cash amounting to $219." "That means that the master organizer is holding the funds for his outlaws. We'll get most of that back, later."

"Now the bounties, the Central Bank is offering $1,000 per outlaw and $2,000 for the master organizer. Murdock and another outlaw also had private bounties on their heads of $1,500 and $500 respectively. So, here are the Western Union vouchers for $8,000." "Separate the $219 between you and your deputies, a fair pay for your assistance and use of your jail. I will deposit the $8,600 in the Durango National Bank. I will then go to the Central Bank and find out which dead guard or coach driver had dependents they were supporting. If there were, I will take care of them as part of my mission." "I understand."

***

The next day Cal sent two telegrams"

> TO - AMOS FARLEY, SILVER CIRCLE -STOP- AM STILL IN DURANGO-STOP-FROM -CAL HARNELL, DURANGO CO

> TO-CAPTAIN ENNIS, MARSHAL SERVICE, DENVER CO-HAVE CAPTURED SIX OUTLAWS, FOUR HANGED, TWO SHOT DEAD-STOP-KNOW NAME OF MASTER ORGANIZER-STOP-HOLD UP ON SPY ROUNDUP-STOP-TILL ALL OUTLAWS CAPTURED-STOP-FROM-CAL HARNELL, DURANGO CO

That afternoon, the Central Bank Manager, Everett Mercer, asked for a meeting. The parties included: Cliff Monroe of the Durango Coach Line, Perry Cox of Cox Security, Sheriff

Lockwood and Cal. Mr. Mercer pointed out, "there hasn't been a payroll delivery since the last robbery, when a tree was dropped on the stagecoach and a half dozen men were killed. The mines are pushing hard to get a delivery. Is there any way we can risk a delivery?"

Mr. Cox and Monroe both said, "the security guards and coach drivers refuse to man a delivery until the last members of the Benson and Greeley gangs are brought to justice." Sheriff Lockwood added, "since the recent Murdock gang's hanging, the remaining outlaws have disappeared and are likely waiting for a delivery to express their revenge and retribution. It's not safe to proceed at this time. What do you think Deputy Marshal Harnell?"

Cal said, "I agree, we need to remove the remaining six outlaws before the US Marshal Service rounds up the spies and master organizer." The frustrated bank manager said, "and how do you propose we accomplish this, sooner than later?"

"I propose we let it be known that we are organizing a delivery. We need one driver and one shotgun guard, with an empty coach and a fake strongbox. I will scout two miles ahead to find their ambush site. I will then ride back and leave, in the middle of the road, my hat on a stick to stop the stagecoach. I will then go back to the ambush site and engage the outlaws in a gunfight. Your driver and shotgun guard will never be in danger."

Everyone was thinking of Cal's proposal. Mr. Cox and Monroe nodded their heads in agreement, and one said, "your reputation precedes you, and we will be your driver and shotgun guard. Pass the information to the spy ring and let's do it."

***

The next day, the fake coach took off a half hour after Cal and Max were on the road west to Cortez. Cal had traveled some five miles with Max in the lead. Suddenly, Max stopped and froze in his tracks. Cal stepped down and sneaked through the trees to see a tree across the road and the six outlaws hiding behind trees some fifty yards off the road. Cal doubled back a mile and left his hat impaled on a stick as planned. He then rode back and tied Boss to a tree, safe from stray bullets. He then approached amongst the trees till he had a clear view of the outlaws some 200 yards away. He then set his Malcolm 8X scope to 200 yards and yelled, "put your hands up, you're all under arrest."

The outlaws were shocked to hear the order. Their plans had been reversed, and they were now the hunted. The gang responded by firing at Cal. Their 1873 rifles were out of range with bullets falling short of their target. Cal spotted them with his scope and started firing his long- range Winchester 1876 in 45-70 caliber. Two outlaws quickly fell, and the remainder were hunched down behind trees. After waiting, Cal sent Max with the order to attack. Max sneaked behind boulders and suddenly attacked one of the outlaws. Mayhem broke out with an outlaw trying to fend off a mad dog. Cal saw another outlaw come to his friend's help, but he picked him off before he could shoot Max.

To Cal's surprise, two of the outlaws were seen escaping on their horses, and leaving their partner fighting and screaming at Max. Cal could not get a shot at them, so he started to walk towards the battle. Suddenly, the outlaw got up and drew his pistol to shoot Max. Cal quickly got a shot off and nearly decapitated the outlaw with a neck shot.

Realizing that two outlaws were getting away, Cal ran back to pick up his horse. To his surprise the stagecoach was arriving next to Boss. Cal said, "what are you doing here?" "Mr. Cox said, "with all the shooting, we didn't feel right leaving you alone, so we decided to come and join in the fight." "Well, there are four dead outlaws, and two have escaped. Max and I are going after them. Please pick up the outlaws, their guns and trail their horses back to Durango. I'll be back with the other two and put an end to this caper."

Meanwhile, the two gang leaders, Benson and Greeley, had pushed their horses at a full gallop for five minutes, and had to stop to allow their horses to blow. While waiting, Benson asked what their plan should be. Greeley said, "we are heading to Cortez where we can hide in a big town. We are forty miles away and won't be able to make it today since it's late in the day. We'll stop on the way and get supplies for a cold camp. In the morning we'll make it to Cortez." "Do you think that lawman will come after us?" "No, but we'll keep watching our backtrail for a dust cloud."

Cal brought Max to the gunfight site, so Max could get a scent to follow. Getting on the trail, Max took the lead. Cal expected the outlaws would stay on the road, but with Max leading, they would not miss a turn if they started to go cross-country.

Cal arrived at a small unnamed town and went to the mercantile. He asked the owner, "has two men, riding through, stopped here within the past hour?" "Yes, they bought a can of beans, cheese, crackers, beef jerky and two bottles of whiskey. They looked like they had been riding hard. They paid for their goods and I saw them heading west out of town." "Thank you." "You're welcome, and by the way, it's going to get cold and snow tonight. Hope you have a winter coat?" "I do."

Meanwhile, Benson and Greeley were in camp, getting cold and drinking whiskey. Benson said, "we never saw a dust cloud and it's too damn cold and wet to go without a fire. Let's start one and get comfortable in our rain slickers." Greeley responded, "I agree."

Cal got back on the trail, at a very slow trot, to allow Max to find the turn off for the outlaw's camp. It got colder and started snowing. Cal put his winter coat on. After riding an hour, Max stopped and started circling the bushes till he found the outlaw's trail. Cal walked Boss behind Max till they could smell wood smoke from a camp fire. He then tied Boss to a tree and walked the rest of the way with his shotgun in his hands.

Cal and Max snuck up to within twenty-five yards without the outlaws detecting their approach. Benson was standing adding wood to the fire, when Cal said to Max, "run, jump and attack. Max took three long strides and went airborne, landing his 90 pounds on Benson's back. Benson went flying and smacked his head on a tree stump. With Benson out, Max turned around and grabbed Greeley's rump. Greeley never got his pistol out. Instead, he was screaming and hopping about like a chicken without a head. The more Greeley tried to swat Max off, the tighter his jaw was clamping on his rump. After due punishment, Cal called Max off. "If you don't want any more, better put your hands up and turn around." Greeley had no choice with Max growling at him and Cal holding a shotgun on him. Cal then manacled both outlaws to a tree and went back to get Boss.

Upon his return to camp, he placed a cervical collar and chained it to the tree. He then changed the tree/wrist manacles, to putting their hands in their backs and manacled them in place. With Benson finally waking up, he checked their pockets and relieved them of $489 in cash which he pocketed. He then removed their boots and found one derringer and one knife. He replaced their boots and walked away. In the saddlebags he found cheese, crackers and one can of beans. Max got the beef jerky. Cal opened the can of beans and warmed it by the fire, while he snacked on the cheese and crackers.

After a nice dinner, Benson yelled out, "hey, we are cold, thirsty, hungry and need to pee." Cal got up and walked up to them, and without any warning he cut and tore the rain slickers off their backs. Then saying, "now you can add wet to your demands. If I hear one more word from you, you're going to lose some teeth. You murderers are finally going to be erased from humanity, and I have no urge to make you comfortable. So, shut up and let me sleep."

Cal built up the fire, put his bedroll out and covered it with a waterproof tarp. Max got under the tarp and settled down for the night. During the night, Benson yells out, "hey lawman, we've got to go pee."

Cal got up, grabbed a piece of firewood, and went to Benson. He smacked him in the mouth. Blood and teeth were spitting out of his mouth and he peed himself. Greeley thought that was funny, so Cal gave him the same treatment and the result was the same. The remainder of the night was quiet.

The next day, shivering outlaws appreciated the short ride to Durango. Sheriff Lockwood greeted Cal and said, "I knew you'd come back with these two, but didn't think they would be alive. Judge Stanley added, "this is good for the town's morale. We will have a trial tonight and I'll get to sentence them if found guilty."

"Please delay the trial till tomorrow. Let me arrest the spies and the master organizer, so we can add them as defendants. If we are lucky we may get the spies to implicate the organizer." "Heck, that's even better, can you apprehend them today, so the prosecutor can offer a reduced sentence if someone identifies the master organizer?" "Yes, with the sheriff's help, we can do this now." "I'm with you, let's go."

Cal went to his saddlebags, pulled out a folded paper signed by Captain Ennis, and handed it to Sheriff Lockwood. He read three names: Walter and Brad Cummings, and Wilhem Hocksler esq. Sheriff Lockwood says,

"Walter Cummings works at the Central Bank and lives with his brother, Brad. Hocksler is an attorney in town who always seems to be defending outlaws and be involved with shady deals. Guess their clock has just stopped, let's go get them." Judge Stanley issued three arrest warrants and handed them to the sheriff.

Cal and the sheriff entered the Central Bank and were greeted by Mr. Mercer. "What can I do for you gents?" "We are here to arrest the spy who has been informing the outlaws of your shipments." "Are you saying it's one of my employees?" "You got it right!" As Cal steps up to Walter Cummings and says, "you are under arrest for being an accessory to robbery and murder and may Judge Stanley have mercy on you." Cummings turned pale and started trembling as the manacles were applied. He kept saying, "I want a lawyer."

On way to the jail, they stopped at Brad's apartment. When Brad opened the door, he saw his brother in manacles. In response, he slammed the door in the sheriff's face and ran to the rear door entrance. Unfortunately, Cal was standing in the doorway, and slammed a full fist punch into his nose and flattened him to the floor.

After leaving the boys in jail, they went to Hocksler's office, and entered without knocking. Hocksler yelled out, "you have no right to enter my office without a warrant." "my pleasure," as he handed the paper. Hocksler read the warrant and nearly collapsed on his desk. The sheriff added, "you have to be one stupid smart ass to think you could get away with this caper," as he applied the manacles.

Cal then adds, "unless I'm wrong, all the stolen money is in this safe, heh! What is the combination?" "Never in my lifetime and this is an impregnable vault, so screw you." Cal didn't even hesitate, he propped Hocksler on the desk, straddled his chest and opened his mouth. Unceremoniously, he shoved the awl in a molar's black center. The sheriff even turned pale as Hocksler stiffened and howled like a dying wolf. Cal relented when Hocksler passed out. He slapped his face to regain consciousness and showed him the awl. "Do you want another dose in another tooth?" "42-14-91."

Sheriff Lockwood opened the vault and pulled out US currency totaling $69,000. "Well, Mr. Mercer might be happy to get this money back on behalf of his parent company." "Isn't it strange that he only offered $2,000 for the capture of the gang's organizer. He didn't offer any reward for the return of the stolen money?" "No, but let me see what I can get out of him?"

Cal and the sheriff went to see Mr. Mercer. "How come you are not offering a reward for the return of the money?" "For two reasons, I didn't think the money would ever be recovered, and 60% of the money is insured by 'Lloyd's of London.'" "How much have you lost and what reward do you offer?" "We lost $70,000 and I'll offer a 10% reward for the return of any amount up to $70,000." "Well, in that case, make me a voucher for $6,900 and we'll apply it to Cal's fund to help the victims of these crimes."

That afternoon, the county prosecutor,

Leopold Parker, visited with the Cummings. He offered them a fifteen-year sentence if they would name the gang organizer and agree with the sentence without a trial. They jumped on the great deal and avoided hanging, but guaranteed Hocksler would hang instead of getting off on a technicality from a shrewd lawyer.

At 9AM, the trial was held. Benson, Greeley, and Hocksler were all found guilty and sentenced to hang at dusk. Everyone in Durango and many local miners attended the hangings—for closure on the matter.

The next day, the sheriff did a settlement of Cal's earnings. "First, I distributed the $6,900 reward amongst heirs of the murdered security guards and drivers. I also found out that only one heir had dependents. Mrs. Samuels has two teenage daughters and has minimal income." "Not a problem, I'll take care of Mrs. Samuels." "Ok, well here's how the funds were distributed. Two livery hostlers bid for the six horses and tack. They bought three each for a total of $450. The local gunshop bought six pistols and six rifles for $300.

The pocket cash out of all the outlaws, spies, and Hocksler totaled $400. The Central Bank parent company's reward for six outlaws and two spies was $8,000. The private bounty on Benson and Greeley was $3,000. The extra reward for Hocksler was $2,000. The total is $13,750 and I have Western Union vouchers for that amount made out to you." "Thank you and keep the pocket cash for you and your deputies. I hope you will watch over Mrs. Samuels because as a widow, she will need protection, if you follow my drift." "I think Mrs. Samuels is a special person, and I'll keep my eye on her, if you follow my drift, heh!"

After making a large deposit at the local commercial bank, he arranged for a bank transfer to his account at the Denver National Bank. To the bank's presidents surprise he excluded $6,000 and started an account in the name of Sandra J Samuels.

Cal then used every resource possible and dug up what was known about Sandra Samuels. For lunch, he went to Gretchen's diner. As he entered he saw a two mid sixties cooking team. He sat down and had the chicken and dumplings special. After the meal, he handed the waitress a silver dollar and asked to speak to the owner. An elderly man came to his table and said, "I'm Gretchen's husband, Al, was there a problem with your dinner?" "No sir, it was wonderful. Why are you still working at your age?" "You're right, we are too old to maintain this pace. Our son, the lawyer in Colorado Springs, has built us a grandparent addition to his house and we are planning to move as soon as we sell the diner. The diner includes the apartment upstairs with three bedrooms and living quarters." "Would you be willing to work with a new owner for the next two weeks?" "Of course." "How much do you want?" "Because it is a profitable business, centrally located in town and of course across the street from the hotel and the sheriff's office, we would like $3,000." "Sold," as he hands Al a bank draft for $3,000 and adds, "I'll be back for dinner with the new owners. Something tells me you will be pleased with that family."

That afternoon, Cal went to see Mrs. Samuels. After introductions were made, Cal sat with Sandra, the two daughters, and the topic lead to finances. "Would you tell me what you have for income?" "I just received $575 from Sheriff Lockwood, my share of the twelve murdered guards and drivers. To support myself and two daughters, I work part-time at Gretchen's diner. However, the place is going up for sale and there is no guarantee that my services will be needed by the new owner. My only skill is cooking and there are few jobs available in this market."

Cal said, "enough said, here is something for you." Sandra looks at the paper, a bank account with a balance of $3,000. Sandra is shocked, and says, "what is this for?" "You are a victim and you need some justice. You lost your husband and will likely lose your job. With two teenage girls, you need some form of financial support. I have bought Gretchen's diner and the deed was put in your name. It also includes the upstairs apartment—your new home. You can be the cook and your daughters can be your assistants or waitresses. It follows the philosophy, 'instead of feeding you a basket of fish, I will teach you how to fish and never worry about you going hungry!'"

Mrs. Samuels was crying and said, "but why you? I don't even know you." "I am the bounty hunter/deputy US marshal that captured the outlaws who killed your husband. I avenged your husband's murder and I will assist you financially as well as offer you protection from those men who would take advantage of a widow." "For protection, I am giving you a double barrel shotgun and a Webley Bulldog pistol. Sheriff Lockwood has agreed to teach you their proper use. I will also promise you that if you ever need me, just notify Amos Farley in Silver Circle and label it urgent. I will return on the next train."

"Now let's all go for dinner. Al and Gretchen need to meet the new owners. They will stay with you for two weeks to get you up to snuff as the cook and new owner." "How do I ever thank you?" "By continuing to live."

With the assignment completed, Cal sent a telegram to Captain Ennis:

> TO: CAPTAIN ENNIS, US MARSHAL SERVICE, DENVER CO-STOP-ASSIGNMENT COMPLETED AND CASE CLOSED-STOP-DO I HEAD FOR DENVER-STOP-OR WAIT FOR YOUR CALL?-STOP-FROM: CAL HARNELL, DEPUTY US MARSHAL, DURANGO CO

Cal paid for the telegram and paid the telegrapher to send his response of the saloon next door and later at the hotel across the street. Cal had just finished his two beers when a telegraph messenger handed him the answer:

> TO: DEPUTY US MARSHAL HARNELL-DURANGO, CO-STOP-HAVE MAJOR ISSUE ON NORTH EASTERN PLAINS-STOP-COME STRAIGHT TO DENVER-STOP-ASAP. FROM:

CAPTAIN ENNIS, US MARSHAL SERVICE, DENVER CO.

Arranging for passage on the ten-hour train ride, Cal never realized that this next assignment would change his life forever.

***

CHAPTER 4— Northeastern Plains

After several train changes, railroad yard meals and some ten hours later, Cal arrived in Denver. He then walked his two horses to the railroad livery and then took a buggy taxi to the US Marshal Service. Leaving Max on the boardwalk, he entered the lobby and was greeted by a new clerk who introduced himself as Deputy Marshal Steve Lions. "I'm Cal Harnell and have a meeting with the Captain."

"Welcome, and Captain Ennis is waiting for you. Follow me."

"Hello Cal, I just got a nice telegram, from Sheriff Lockwood praising your activity in capturing the outlaws in Durango. Now I want to hear the blow by blow plays from arrival to departure." Half an hour later, Cal had pretty much covered all the salient aspects.

"That was a nice job. You saved the public, coach drivers, and guards from further harm, helped the families of fallen members, returned the stolen money, and provided justice for Mrs. Samuels."

"Now, what is going on to bring me here so soon?"

"Range wars between cattle ranchers and sheep farmers. This problem started in Wyoming, but the sheepherders have now moved south to our bordering plains. I now have six deputies in the Northwestern Plains dealing with the disputes and cannot spare any for the beginning problem in the Northeastern Plains. What do you know about sheepherding and the current problems?"

"Nothing, please enlighten me!"

"Historically, sheepherding was a nomadic enterprise, where sheepherders were sharing the open-range with cattle ranchers. Over years of ill feelings, the ranchers are now fencing their lands with barb- wire. The sheepherding industry is now changing to a domestic farming method by owning their own ranges and fencing them off with mesh fences. The current problem arises when a cattle rancher wants to expand his grazing lands. They are pushing the sheep farmers to sell their lands by putting them out of business. We now have a modern war of sheep being slaughtered, fences being torn down and herds being scattered in an attempt to bankrupt the sheep farmers, forcing them to sell their land and homesteads. Things have recently gotten worse with sheep farmers being shot to death."

"This is where you come in. In Plainville, Sheriff Howard Lovering is requesting assistance to stop the killings. There is a large rancher who is suspect, but the sheriff does not have the manpower to arrest him. He needs your help. This is a dangerous assignment because the cattle rancher has hired two Regulators. These use to function by catching cattle thieves, but now they are nothing but assassins. Unfortunately, these Regulators are also professional gunfighters, and that is why we are asking you for your help. If you accept, talk to Sheriff Lovering before you start your investigation. The Sheepherding Association has put a $2,000 reward for the capture of the murderers. We also believe the Regulators have a price on their heads."

Cal accepted the assignment. He picked up basic supplies for a week. Took the train to Fort Morgan with his horses and Max. Arriving in Fort Morgan, he picked up Boss, Buster and Max. To get familiar with the eastern grasslands, he wanted to get a view of the area by riding on horseback. By the time he traveled half way to Plainville, all he saw were large cattle ranches, half of which were fenced in. At nightfall, he set up camp. He started a fire and had a fried potato and beefsteak dinner, fresh supplies he had added in Fort Morgan. Max got the bone.

The next day, the last twenty miles to Plainville revealed a different landscape. Cal saw sheep ranches interspersed with cattle ranches. All ranches were fenced in. The sheep ranches used a mesh fence and the cattle ranches were using three or four strands of barbwire. The sheep ranches were also showing signs of cultivation to improve their pastures as well as raising hay for winter feed. The layouts seemed to Cal a solution to the old range wars. Every rancher would now be on his own dedicated and fenced in lands.

Arriving in Plainsville, Cal saw a town of approximately five hundred people. There were plenty of service businesses and the main street was clean. Boardwalks were continuous and the railroad yard hard pens to hold both cattle and sheep. This was a nice appearing town that was well laid out. With the many windmill wells, it was clear that most homes and businesses had cold and hot water for indoor plumbing. Cal went to the Central Hotel, booked a room for a week and housed his horses at Willy's Livery, three buildings away from the hotel. After he was settled in, he and Max went to the sheriff's office.

Once he entered the office, he was greeted by a young deputy. "My name is Deputy Paul Windman, how may I help you?" "I'm Cal Harnell, US Special Deputy Marshal, sent by Captain Ennis to assist your sheriff." "Yes, we have been expecting you, follow me."

Seeing the sheriff, Cal was a bit surprised.

Sheriff Lovering was an older lawman approaching his late sixties. After introductions were made, the sheriff said, "where are your deputies, I was expecting a small army of US Marshals."

"I'm it, so kindly fill me in with the problem at hand."

"If you insist, this is the situation. We have the Rocking W Ranch that is a cattle ranch of twelve sections. That is about eight thousand acres of unimproved range land. The owner is Wilson Whitehouse, the most powerful man in the county. The problem is that he is surrounded by other cattle ranches that have fenced in their lands, and the fenced in lands held by sheep farmers. He wants to expand his herd because of the rising beef prices but cannot get more land since he is surrounded by other ranch's barb wire or sheep fence. Since the surrounding cattle ranchers are his friends, the only way to expand is to purchase sheep farms."

"Ok, but I still don't see what the problem is."

"The problem is that the sheep farmers are not selling. This has started a war. Whitehouse has added more cowboys that know nothing about handling cattle but are good with a gun. He has also added two Regulators. The result is that every night, the sheep farmers are losing a dozen sheep shot by marauders. To make it worse, Mexican workers are being shot at and one landowner was killed. We have plenty of witnesses that will testify against the Regulators who have killed the one landowner. In addition, landowners and their wives have been severely beaten by the hired gunslingers, to convince them to sell. It's a mess and Paul and I are not able to bring these murderers to justice or stop Wilson Whitehouse. Paul has investigated and talked to Wilson Whitehouse. He has denied that he has ordered his men to shoot sheep or the landowners. The Regulators and the gunslingers have also denied any wrong doing. We know they are all lying, but it would be suicide for us to try to arrest any of his men. Can you help us?"

"Yes, I will. Is there one sheep farmer that is a spokesman or leader, that I can speak with?"

"Yes, that would be Levi and Clara Sullivan

at the L-C Connected Ranch. It's situated three miles east of town and the nearest western neighbor to Wilson Whitehouse."

Meanwhile at the Rocking W Ranch, Wilson Whitehouse was meeting with the two Regulators, the two new gunslingers, and his sons Ray and Dan. The subject was Levi Sullivan. Wilson says, "I have discovered that he is the leader of the Sheep Farmers' Union. He has been encouraging the other four farmers west of us to hold on to their farms. We have been eliminating the wrong owners and workers. We must get rid of Sullivan and convince his wife to sell to us. I want one of you Regulators to do the hit and one of you gunslingers to beat the wife till she agrees to sell, today." "Ray adds, "what do you want me to do?" "I want you to wait till tomorrow and then visit the other three farmers. Since they all have one section plus buildings, make them an offer of $5,000, and with Sullivan out of the way, they will likely sell."

Dan joins the discussion, "pa, you know I've been against this war from the start, now I hear there have been deaths and you are planning another execution today. When is it going to stop? You are all going to get caught and hang for these murders. I want nothing to do with this, and I'm leaving you and this ranch."

"Son, what part of this need do you not understand. We are growing, and we need more land. When we get these ten sections held by the sheep farmers, it will add 7,000 acres and will double the size of this ranch. This is your inheritance, so don't throw it away. It is what it is, and if you leave now, don't plan on coming back."

"I'm leaving, if you change your mind, you can find me at the Central Hotel."

"So be it. Ok, Sweeney and Cooper, you're are up. Get it done."

After leaving the sheriff's office, he picked up Boss and Max, and rode east towards Sullivan's L-C Connected Ranch. Each mile revealed a nice sheep ranch with well kept outbuildings and ranch houses. The ranches were clearly fenced in, and by the size of the bunkhouse, it was clear that several farm hands were employed. Some of the farms even had agricultural implements parked outside the barns. It all voted for well-organized and profitable farming enterprises.

As Cal was approaching the access road for the Sullivan ranch, he rode up to a wagon loaded with supplies. Cal said hello to the Mexican couple and asked them, "is this the Sullivan ranch ahead?" "Yes, senor, I am Pedro Rodriguez, and this is my wife, Elena. I see you are a US Marshall, and Mr. Sullivan will be pleased to see you. Please follow me. You can introduce yourself to Mrs. Sullivan while I get Mr. Sullivan from the pastures."

Arriving in the yard, he tied Boss to the hitch rail and told Max to stay on the porch. He knocked, but no one answered. Seeing the door partially open, he said, "anyone home." As he entered, he saw a naked woman whose dress and underclothing had been ripped off. She was unconscious with multiple facial bruises, a broken nose, bruises over her right chest and several bruises over her abdomen. Worst of all, she was bleeding from her genital area.

Verifying that she was still alive, he yelled to Elena for help. As she entered she placed her hands to her face and said, "Oh Dios mio! Is she alive, senor?"

"Yes, do you have a doctor in Plainsville?'
"Si, we have Doctor Brewster and the Plainsville Hospital."

"In that case, please attend to her bleeding, I will unload the wagon of supplies, add a mattress to the wagon's floor, and we are bringing her to the hospital." While preparations were underway, Pedro arrived with the bad news that he had found Mr. Sullivan shot dead. Meanwhile, Elena had washed Mrs. Sullivan of the blood and applied a Hoosier belt. Pedro then helped Cal load their patient to the wagon and Elena stayed by Mrs. Sullivan's side. On leaving, Cal said, "Pedro, I will send Sheriff Lovering and the undertaker."

The ride to Plainsville was brisk at a medium trot. Once in town, seeing the sheriff sitting on the boardwalk, Cal yells out, "Sheriff, please follow us to the hospital." Cal drove the team next to the emergency entrance and was met by two nurses pushing a wheeled bed. They transferred Mrs. Sullivan and Doc Brewster asked who he was and what happened?

"I'm Cal Harnell, a US Deputy Marshall, investigating the death of sheep farmers. When I went to interview the Sullivan's, I found this naked lady unconscious, with evidence of a beating, as well as bleeding from her genital area. Also, sad to say, but her husband is dead from a gunshot wound."

"Very well Marshal, let me examine her and I will tell you what I find and what I can do."

Cal waited with Sheriff Lovering. The sheriff agreed he would go investigate the death scene and the undertaker would bring back Mr. Sullivan's body. As they were talking, Doc Brewster came to the waiting area. "This lady has a serious concussion, a fractured nose, many facial bruises and three broken ribs. She is bleeding in her right chest and I'll have to insert a chest tube to drain her right chest. The abdominal bruises have not just started her monthly but caused her to have an early miscarriage. Plus, she has been tortured beyond the obvious beating, she has two broken fingers and a broken left forearm. Assuming she survives, she may be a hospital resident for weeks."

"Doc, please do everything you can for her, and I will cover all financial costs." "Of course, please come back in a couple of hours for more information." Meanwhile, Pedro arrived, and Cal asked him to gather the other sheep farm owners/managers and set up a meeting at the sheriff's office. Sheriff Lovering then added, "we know who is responsible but cannot arrest anybody unless Mrs. Sullivan can identify her attacker by name."

"I agree, but that doesn't mean I can't meet with Whitehouse and tell him, he and his men are suspects. In addition, I have a plan to protect the sheep and the workers until I arrest or kill those responsible."

While waiting for Doc Brewster, Cal walked to the telegraph office and sent a gram to an old friend in Boulder.

TO: ERIC ALDERSON, RAINBOW AGENCY, BOULDER CO. NEED TEN GUARDS TO WORK DAWN TO DAWN-STOP-TO PROTECT SHEEP AND THEIR WORKERS-STOP-WILL PAY $5 PER 12 HOUR SHIFT-STOP-NEED HELP NOW-STOP-

FROM: CAL HARNELL, DEPUTY US MARSHAL, PLAINSVILLE HOSPITAL, PLAINSVILLE CO.

Cal paid for the gram and for any answer to be brought to the hospital, urgently. He then returned to the hospital and waited for more news on Mrs. Sullivan's condition. Doc Brewster came from the operating room and said, "the chest drainage procedure went well, I have repositioned her nose and splinted her broken bones, and her miscarriage has completed. She is still unconscious, and I would like someone to sit with her until she wakens. The only unknown factor is what damage she has had to her brain, if any. If and when she wakens, we will know and hopefully she can identify her attackers. She is still in our recovery room and will be there at least another three hours."

Cal says, "I'll be the one to sit by her. I have some business to take care of but will be back by the time you release her to her room."

Cal was stepping up to Boss when the telegraph messenger arrived. He read the message:

TO: Cal HARNELL, PLAINSVILLE HOSPITAL, PLAINSVILLE CO

TEN AGENTS ARRIVING BY 5PM TODAY-STOP-WILL STAY AS LONG AS NECESSARY.

FROM: ERIC ALDERSON, RAINBOW AGENCY, BOULDER CO

Cal and Max rode off to the Rocking W Ranch. He traveled the eight miles in one hour. Arriving at the access road, he rode under the gate and stopped at the main house. He stepped down and was greeted by a cowhand sitting on the porch.

"Who are you and what brings you to the Rocking W?"

"I'm Cal Harnell, Deputy US Marshall. And who are you?"

"I'm Ray Whitehouse."

"I see, I'm here to see your father."

"Very well, follow me!" After entering the house and moving to the office, Ray said, "Pa, this man says he's a US Marshall and wants to see you."

Without any greeting, Whitehouse says in a gruff and demeaning voice, "what in hell do you want?"

"I'm here to put an end to the sheep wars you are responsible for. Today, someone killed Levi Sullivan and beat Mrs. Sullivan to within an inch of her life. Yet she survived and when she awakens, she will identify her attacker and her husband's killer. I will then be back here to arrest you and the culprits, and that's a promise."

"You and what army. When you come back you'll be facing a dozen of my men."

"The more the better for the undertaker." Cal had not realized that Ray was standing behind him. As Ray put his hand on his pistol, Max took a good bite of his gun hand. Ray screamed and held his bleeding hand as Max continued to growl. As Cal departed, he added, "I'm placing security guards at each of the sheep farms. So, tell your marauders that they can expect lead coming at them. Their orders are to shoot to kill."

As Cal was leaving he added, "if I disappear or am found shot dead, Captain Ennis will be visiting you with an army of US Marshals. That's going to be a real memorable event, heh?"

As Cal arrived in town, he stopped at the sheriff's office to have a meeting with the sheep owners/managers. He informed them that they would all have security guards for their protection. Each farm would have two guards to cover 24 hours a day, to protect the workers and prevent nighttime slaughtering of sheep. Their only costs would be to provide the guards room and board in the bunkhouse.

After the meeting, Cal anticipated a long wait for the patient to awaken, so he left Boss and Max at Willey's Livery. Entering the hospital, Mrs. Sullivan was moved to a private room and Cal started his vigil.

Cal stayed by her side, initially mesmerized by the extent of tubes and bottles attached to her chest to catch blood and release escaping air. He commented to the nurse, that only years ago, anyone with this chest injury would certainly have died. During mealtime, Cal was relieved by either the sheriff or his deputy. Whitehouse's spies needed to verify that this woman was protected by the law.

Getting a late dinner at Ginny's Diner, Cal had company. Ten well-armed men arrived looking for Cal. Introductions were done, and Cal invited all ten men to a free dinner. Waiting for their meal, Cal explained the politics of the war and the damages already incurred. They were informed to shoot to kill anyone killing sheep or shooting at workers.

After dinner, Cal went back to Mrs. Sullivan's room to find Doc Brewster leaning over the patient and saying, "Clara, you've known me since you were born, and you know I always speak the truth. I'm so sad to say that Levi is dead and that you have miscarried. Clara cried and cried for almost an hour, and then seemed to fall in a deep hole. Cal was sitting by her side and eventually spoke up.

"Mrs. Sullivan, I'm Cal Harnell, Deputy US Marshall. My condolences for your losses, and I'm here to offer you my help to find justice."

"Well Marshal, I suspect you aren't aware of the difficulty we sheep farmers face, and you don't know me. So, why and how can you help?"

"Why, because it's my mission as a bounty hunter and Deputy Marshall to help victims, and with your losses, you are a victim. How, by avenging your husband's death and bringing the murderer to trial. This is crucial, did you recognize the men who beat you and killed your husband?"

"Yes, I was sitting in my main room sewing when I heard hoofbeats. I looked out of the window and saw the Regulator and the new gunslinger from the Rocking W Ranch. The Regulator was named Sweeney and the gunfighter was named Cooper. As they approached the house, Sweeney turned his horse and headed for the pasture where Levi was herding the flock. Cooper stopped at the house, tied his horse at the hitching rail, and stepped on the porch."

Sweeney and Cooper never realized that someone else was watching, with field glasses, the Sullivan homestead.

"Without knocking, Cooper pushed through the door, got in my face, and started to yell at me."

"Mr. Whitehouse is making you his final offer of $5,000 for your herd and farm. Sign this bill of sale or suffer the consequences."

"When I refused to sign, he slapped me in the face, and I fought back by scratching his left face. He lost control from my attack, punched me in the nose with a full fist, and knocked me to the floor. He then kicked me in the chest and abdomen several times. When I again refused to sign the sales contract, he broke two of my fingers and snapped my forearm. When I again refused to sign, he punched me in the face several times till everything went black. Now I find myself in the hospital with you at my side. I may also add that when he was kicking me, I heard a gunshot and knew that Levi was dead."

"If you're willing to swear to this in a court of law, I will go and arrest those two, today. While I'm gone, Sheriff Lovering and his deputy will stand guard to protect you from Whitehouse's toadies."

Cal arrived at the Rocking W Ranch at noon. He stopped at the main house knowing that Whitehouse would be in his office eating his lunch. Knocking on the door, his son Ray answered the door. His response was, "get out of here." Cal never hesitated, he drew his pistol and walked Ray to his pa's office. "How dare you pull a gun on my son and barge in my office?"

"Shut up and listen to me. I'm here on official US Marshal business to arrest your new man, by the name of Sweeney, for murder. I am also arresting your cowhand or gunslinger by the name of Cooper for aggravated assault." "Ray, go to the bunkhouse and fetch these two men." "If you come back with more than these two, I will arrest both of you with a charge of interfering with a lawman and obstructing justice."

As Sweeney and Cooper arrived in the office. Cal arrested Cooper who denied the charge, saying that he was in the bunkhouse when the attack happened. When asked how he got the facial scratches, he said, that he rubbed too close to a tree branch. When confronted with the fact that the victim was alive and had fingered him for the beating, he stopped objecting. Manacles were applied with his hands in his back.

Things were different with Sweeney. Cal charged him for the murder of Levi Sullivan. He also said he had an alibi, working the range with a half dozen cowboys. Cal informed him of two facts: the victim saw him arrive with Cooper and also saw him head out to the pastures where Levi was working.

Sweeney knew he was in trouble and decided he would not allow being arrested.

Without a moment's hesitation, he went for his gun. Cal knew he would challenge him and saw Sweeney go for his gun. Cal drew his Colt and fired before Sweeney finished clearing leather. The powerful 44-40 bullet hit Sweeney in the right shoulder joint and shattered the arm bone and shoulder assembly. The bullet impact turned him half circle and he ended up falling to his knees. Cal immediately put the manacles on him as Sweeney screamed, moaned and called Cal every vile expletive in his vocabulary.

Cal then gave the Whitehouse's the option. "Try to stop me from leaving with these two criminals and you will also get arrested or get shot in the process. Your choice!" Whitehouse raised his hands and said, "I wouldn't ever consider going against a US Marshal."

As Cal was going back to Plainsville with his caravan, Whitehouse sent Ray to the bunkhouse to bring his other Regulator and gunfighter, Shelby and Palmer.

Whitehouse starts, "we have a problem. Sweeney and Cooper have been arrested for murder and aggravated assault. The only witness against them is Clara Sullivan who is in the Plainsville Hospital. She needs to be silenced now and quietly before she is released from the hospital. Take care of this problem tonight."

"Consider it done, Boss."

Cal arrived in town, knowing the sheriff and deputy were guarding Mrs. Sullivan, he headed for the hospital. Sheriff Lovering took possession of the prisoners, after Cal described the events at the Rocking W Ranch. Cal would write his statement and talk to the prosecutor at a later time.

Cal explained to Doc Brewster how the two criminals were in jail and explained that there may be an attempt on Mrs. Sullivan's life. Doc Brewster said, "she cannot be released with the chest tube apparatus still in place. That could take two more days. So, let's move her to the security room with thick wooden walls that would stop a bullet and not danger the other patients. That's assuming that you will stay with her."

"I'll be here 24 hours a day, except for mealtime when the Sheriff will replace me. If you allow it, Max my guard dog, will be with me also."

"Very well, let's move her and Max can join you all."

That afternoon Mrs. Sullivan was talkative, and Cal was receptive.

"So, you brought back Sweeney and Cooper to stand trial. That now means that my life is in danger. I'm the only witness against them, so if they bump me off, they go free!"

"Yes, but that's not going to happen. I'll be here all afternoon, at dinner, the sheriff will replace me. After dinner, I'm coming back with my partner, Max and we are both spending the night in this room. So, to pass the time, please tell me about yourself."

"I have had a simple background. My dad was foreman on the sheep farm adjacent to ours. How he managed to save money I'll never know. Yet he managed to send me to a one-year business and accounting school. When I graduated, I was hired by the Sullivan farm to care for the books, handle business transactions, documents and communications."

"Within a year, Mr. Sullivan passed away, Levi became owner, and I ended up marrying him, of course. Levi and I were in the process of modernizing the sheep operations by fencing our land into rotating pastures, adding phosphate to the over grazed land, and cultivating areas to grow our own winter feed, to include hay, oats and sugar beets. We were even planning to cultivate the pastures to improve the quality of grazing lands. And that brings me to now—in a hospital bed. Enough of my story, what about you Marshal?"

"My story is much simpler. Ever since I was nineteen years old, I have been working and living with guns. I worked in a gun-shop and learned to perform gun repairs and was trained in the art of fast draw. I then spent a year with a well-established bounty hunter, Amos Farley. When Amos retired, a well know paladin bounty hunter sent me to see Captain Ennis of the US Marshal Service. With a good recommendation from him, I became a US Deputy Marshal. Over the past two years, I have accumulated a sizeable bank account from the rewards on these criminal's heads. I am using this account to fund my victim fund. which I'm using to support the dependent victims of violent crimes."

"Can you give me an example how you have used this fund to help someone in need?"

"Certainly, without mentioning names or locations, I recently help a widow with two daughters. Her husband, a bank clerk, was killed during a robbery. This lady, a housewife, had no source of income to support herself and kids. I purchased a diner and placed her as the cook, owner, and even provided a home in the apartment above the diner. This plus a bank account gave her independence for life."

"So, you avenge their loss, support them financially as needed and anything else?"

"Yes, I offer them protection. I arm them and train them how to use their firearms. Most important, I offer them personal protection for life. If ever they fear for their life, I will come to assist them no matter where I am in this state."

Suddenly someone knocked at the door. Sheriff Lovering announced himself and said, "break and dinner time. I see we have moved to the security room. Do you expect repercussions from Whitehouse?"

"Never know but stay alert, I'll be back shortly."

Cal had a nice dinner of meatloaf, mashed potatoes, carrots, coffee, and a dessert of apple pie. As he was finishing his meal, one of the ten security guards showed up to report on the day's activities. Things were quiet, and the leader wanted to be sure Cal wanted to continue the expensive security detail. "Without a doubt, as a matter of fact, here is $250 which should cover five days. I expect that this caper will be resolved by then. Let's talk again by the end of these five days."

On his way to the hospital, Cal stopped at Willey's Livery and picked up his sawed-off shotgun and Max. Max had no idea where he was going. When they got to the hospital, Max was having trouble handling all the different smells he had never encountered. As he got to Mrs. Sullivan's room, the patient started laughing when she realized who Max was—the

Marshal's partner. Max was brought to the patient, Cal said, "friend and guard." Max stepped up to get his head rubbed and Mrs. Sullivan complied. In turn, Max licked her hand. Cal added, "Ma'am you are now Max's friend for life. He will protect you forever."

As the sheriff was leaving he added, I just received these two Western Union vouchers on Sweeney and Cooper. He hands the vouchers, Cal looks at them, and places them in his pant's rear pocket.

"Well Mr. Marshall, you come back from dinner with your guard dog and a sawed-off shotgun. Guess I'm in more danger than I thought I was, heh?"

"No, the danger is the same. However, do you mind calling me Cal?" "Only if you call me Clara." "Done, Clara. I have ten men protecting your neighbors and your farm. If I didn't think I could not protect you, I would have some of those guards join us."

"In that case, do you mind if I take a short nap. The dinner meal has brought on some fatigue."

"Go ahead, I'll be here when you awaken, and we can continue talking. I really want to know about sheep farming."

Cal was sitting across the door but the other side of the bed behind Clara. Max was next to the foot of the bed but out of view of the door. Clara was sleeping soundly when Max got up and started to growl. Cal told Max to wait. Suddenly the door handle turned and started to open. In entered a white uniformed nurse with a piece of crap cowboy holding a knife to her throat. The second man, holding a knife in his hand, rushed the bed ready to slash Clara's throat.

Things happened quickly. Clara opened her eyes and saw the knife coming at her. Cal did not hesitate. With a full load of #3 Buckshot, Cal pulled both triggers. The outlaw was lifted off his feet and hurled backwards through the door and down the stairs, head over heels.

At the same time, he orders Max to attack. Max jumps up and muckles on to the calf of the man threatening the nurse. The attacker howled in pain and dropped the knife. The nurse escaped his grasp and the attacker was screaming in pain as Max was tearing his skin and muscles. Cal stepped up to the battle and popped the shotgun's butt to his forehead. He collapsed to the floor and the threat was neutralized.

With the room still covered with the shotgun's black smoke, Doc Brewster rushed in the room to see the aftermath. Cal said, "I'm sorry that this happened, but it was a good idea to move us to the third floor away from other residents. Since they are coming for Clara while in the hospital, I will move two guards to the hospital's front and rear entrances—twenty-four hours a day."

Having heard the gunshot, Sheriff Lovering and Deputy Windman arrived shortly. Clara identified the two attackers. "The dead one, at the bottom of the stairs was the Regulator, Shelby, and the one on the floor was the new gunslinger, Palmer. Shelby's body was removed, and Palmer had manacles applied. After he awoke, Doc Brewster examined Max's work and said, "this one needs some wound irrigation and sutures, we don't want him to die of blood poisoning before the trial. So, sheriff, bring him to my treatment room before he's jailed."

As everyone was leaving, the nurse prisoner thanked Cal and especially recognized Max by rubbing his head and ears. Max's bobbed tail was wagging and pounding the floor, as if to say, "you're welcome."

Clara finally spoke up, "I never thought Whitehouse would ever send killers while I'm here. What's it going to be like when I get home?"

"Today, I'm moving all my Rainbow Security Guards to the hospital. I'm then bringing Shelby back to the Rocking W Ranch and arresting Wilson Whitehouse for ordering Levi's murder and the attempted murder on you. After your discharge, I'm keeping the ten private security guards at your ranch till this mess is officially resolved."

"Where are you getting any witnesses against Whitehouse?"

"Today, before I go to get Whitehouse,

I will have two of his hired guns sign a statement implicating Whitehouse as the one who ordered the depredations."

"How are you going to get those two gunslingers to roll over?"

"I have a secret incentive that always works in my favor."

Sheriff Lovering sent his deputy to collect the ten Rainbow guards. With their arrival, five were put to work. Two at the front entrance, two at the rear entrance and one in Clara's room. The other five were sent to the Central Hotel, to book five rooms and get a nap before their shift starts at 8PM till 8AM. Each guard was armed with a double barrel shotgun and their pistol.

Before heading to the Rocking W Ranch, Cal stopped at the jail. He asked Sheriff Lovering and his deputy to step outside and get a coffee at Ginny's Diner. Before leaving, the sheriff manacled Cooper and Palmer to their own cell bars.

As soon as the jail was without witnesses, Cal looked at Cooper and said, "I am certain that if you name the person who ordered you to beat Clara Sullivan, that the prosecutor may be able to negotiate a prison sentence instead of hanging. What do you say?"

"Go to hell, I'll take my chances at trial. If I squeal, I'm dead anyways."

Cal did not hesitate, he stepped in Cooper's cell, opened his mouth and shoved the awl into a juicy cavity. Cooper had a moment when the earth stopped rotating. He then had a major epileptic convulsion and collapsed. After Cooper regained consciousness, Cal said, "what do you say now, or do you want some more dental care?"

"Wilson Whitehouse.... send the prosecutor with a deal and I'll sign."

Cal then went into Palmer's cell, pointed the awl, and asked him what his pleasure was. Palmer said, "I'm only going to be charged with aggravated assault, so go bark-up another tree."

Cal just forced his mouth open and shoved the awl home. Palmer had a moment of silence followed by a scream from hell. As Cal was jiggling the awl, Palmer vomited all over himself. Out of sympathy, Cal offered Palmer some water to rinse his mouth. He accepted, but when the cold water hit the tooth with an opened nerve root, Palmer lost control and wet himself.

Cal then added, "Palmer, you'll have a choice when the prosecutor comes to offer you a deal. Keep in mind that Whitehouse will then be in the adjoining cell, so he won't be a threat and he won't be doing anything to help you. He'll likely put all the blame on you! A deal is for your benefit, and it's going to be the only one you'll get."

"On second thought, a deal sounds good. Send the prosecutor to see me with a deal."

Cal then went to Ginny's Diner and had an early lunch. He told Sheriff Lovering that Palmer had vomited and wet himself, requiring some cleaning up. Also, both men wanted to see the prosecutor to implicate Wilson Whitehouse. Sheriff Lovering asked if there was any evidence of torture. Cal said, "no, but don't offer either some cold water for a few days."

Cal and Max were at Willey's Livery getting ready to leave when an unarmed man walked in. "Marshal, my name is Dan Whitehouse, and may I have a word with you regarding my pa and brother?"

"Certainly, although I need to tell you that I'm on my way to deliver the dead Regulator, Shelby, and to arrest your father for ordering Levi Sullivan's murder and attempted murder of Clara Sullivan."

"I knew that day would come and I'm sad to hear this. I did not know anything of the past deaths since I was against any violence towards sheep farmers. I did however, see Cooper and Sweeney arrive and leave the Sullivan ranch on the day Levi was killed. I even saw you arrive shortly thereafter. I was spying on the ranch with field glasses. I didn't know what Cooper and Sweeney were up to. I would be willing to testify to that fact, if necessary."

"I'll keep that in mind. For now, your pa is looking at prison time. Let's hope your brother puts an end to forcing the sheep farmers out of business. If not, he'll also end up in prison, or dead trying to own their land."

An hour later, Cal, Max and the dead Shelby arrived at the Rocking W Ranch. He rode up to the main house, with his shotgun in hand and Max at his side, he walked inside the house and kicked in the office door. There, standing in total shock, stood Ray, Wilson and another unknown man. Cal said, "who are you?" I'm the ranch foreman, Stuart Wells. As Ray put his hand on his pistol, Max started growling and Ray changed his mind when he saw Max's teeth.

"I'm bringing your killer, Shelby, dead and in your yard. I'm arresting you, Wilson Whitehouse, for ordering the execution of Levi Sullivan and the attempted murder of Clara Whitehouse."

"There's not a jury in this county that will find me guilty without proof."

"I have proof, and you're going to prison. So, turn around and put your hands behind your back. Mr. Wells, please apply the manacles.

Now gentlemen, place your guns on the desk, remove the ammo and let's all step outside." After Whitehouse was helped onto Shelby's freed horse, Cal warns Ray and Stuart, that if they followed him, he would kill them. Whitehouse's departing order to Ray was, "time for Plan B, son."

***

Arriving in Plainsville, Cal dropped Whitehouse at the jail. The sheriff told Cal that Judge Winters has scheduled the trial for two days from now. Cal then added, "I will send four of my security guards to protect the prisoners, Cooper and Palmer, from an early death at the hand of Whitehouse's men."

"That's wise, since both men agreed to the prosecutor's deal. I'm sure that Whitehouse's lawyer will convey to Ray who the witnesses are. Untimely deaths would make it difficult to convict Whitehouse."

Cal then brought Boss and Max to Willy's and sold Shelby's horse and saddle to Willy for $75. He then went back to the hospital. As he entered Clara's room, Clara was sitting in the chair with all tubes out of her chest.

"Hello Cal, I'm so glad to see you. Is Whitehouse in jail?"

"Yes, and the trial is in two days. Will you be able to attend? You won't need to testify since both Cooper and Palmer have accepted a plea deal. They waived their right to a trial and accepted a ten-year prison sentence, in return for a guilty plea and testifying against Whitehouse."

"Yes, Doc Brewster said that, if I don't rebleed in my chest, I can go home the day of the trial. What worries me is what will happen when I get home. I'm certain that Ray Whitehouse will seek revenge against me. My willingness to accuse Cooper and Palmer will lead to Wilson Whitehouse's conviction."

"I'll be staying with you in your house. I will sleep on the main room divan, and I will also have six of the Rainbow Security Guards present on the premises. Three will patrol the house all night, plus we will board-up your bedroom window. You will be safe until we have an agreement with Ray Whitehouse or the culprits are all dead."

"Any agreement must include the right for

sheep farmers to fence-in their property and be allowed to conduct their business without cattlemen trying to bankrupt them. This agreement must be signed by all parties, in the presence of Judge Winters, and at the penalty of fines or imprisonment."

"Agree, now let's talk about a more pleasant subject. I know nothing about sheep farming and would like to know about the business."

"Sheep farming has moved from the original nomadic culture of our Basque ancestors to a homestead business. We now fence-in our land, rotate our grazing pastures, build treatment pens, and build lambing and shearing sheds. We are also planning to cultivate our fields and reseed with hay for improved grazing or harvesting a winter crop. These winter crops would include hay, oats and sugar beets. With improved pastures, we can triple the number of sheep per acre."

"Now for specifics. My farm consists of one section, or 640 acres. I now have 500 Rambouillet sheep that swells to 750 after lambing. These sheep are a common western range breed. I'm now fencing half of my acreage for grazing with a mesh fence, and half for hay with barbwire to keep the neighbor's cattle out. By adding phosphate to replace the lost phosphorous from grazing, I will easily increase my flock to 1000. With cultivated pastures I can increase my flock to 1500-2000."

"Good start now, discuss things like breeding, lambing/tail docking, shearing, expenses and income."

"Breeding occurs in the fall rut season when the ewes come in heat. Each estrus cycle occurs every 17 days. We keep a ram with thirty ewes for two full cycles or 34 days. In cold country, we tend to delay breeding, since a gestation period of five months can lead to early lambing when it's still too cold. By using breeding pens, we prevent breeding at a young age which is a recipe for lambing mortality."

"Lambing is a very busy time. We now use lambing sheds especially for the first-year deliveries. The older ewes do well to deliver in the fields. We need to assist any delivery that lasts more than 45 minutes. Twins are common when the ewes are between the ages of three and six years of age. The assistance we provide is pulling on the lamb and cutting the umbilical cord. We also dock the tail and castrate the selected males at that time."

"Why dock the tail?" "We cut the tail at a level that still covers the anus and vulva. This prevents anal and genitalia diseases, wool maggots, and keeps fecal matter from accumulating on the hindquarter's wool."

"Shearing is a labor-intensive time. It occurs in April before lambing. We shear in the shed where we gather and protect the wool. An experienced shearer can manually shear 30-40 adults per day—or it takes two weeks for one man to shear 500 sheep. After the shearing, we clean, grade and bale the wool into 200-pound bales that we bring by wagon to the rail yard for shipping."

"Our expenses are either labor, winter feed or paying off loans on the buildings. Loans are the only way to pay for the buildings. To handle the workload, we need year-round workers. Our sheep workers live in the bunkhouses with their families. They are faithful workers and we pay them well. We will hire temporary workers to cultivate, plant and harvest crops. Winter feed is very expensive when bought outright. By harvesting our crops, we improve our bottom line, and can increase the number of sheep we can feed during the winter."

"We enjoy income twice a year. In the spring we sell the wool and selected barren ewes for meat. In the fall, we sell lambs for meat and old non-active rams for mutton meat. Meat is based on the age of the sheep. Lamb meat comes from less than a one-year old animal and is the most in demand. Hogget meat comes from an animal between one and two years of age. This meat is darker and a bit more flavorful. Mutton comes from an animal older than two years of age. This can be tough meat that is used in slowly cooked stews. Selling live animals for meat usually yields $8 per animal, depending on weight, age and seasonal rates."

"Wool is our cash crop. An adult sheep can produce an average of 20 pounds of wool. At the current price of 25 cents per pound, each animal can produce an income of $5 per year. Since sheep live to the average age of 12 years, there is a profit to be made."

"That was a nice presentation. Now as a business venture, I'm computing that you are generating approximately $2,500 from wool and $1,500 from meat sales. Assuming that your profit/expense ratio is 60/40, as it is in cattle ranching, then your profit is +-$2,500 per year with 500 sheep +-250 lambs yearly."

"Yes, and since I do the accounting, I can attest to that."

"So, if you double your land holdings, you could technically increase your income to $5,000 per year. Now that is a profitable enterprise."

"That is probably correct. But there is no land for sale that adjoins my land."

"Shall I say that the jury is not out on that yet."

***,

Meanwhile at the Rocking W Ranch, Ray Whitehouse is meeting with Stuart Wells, the ranch foreman. "The trial against pa is tomorrow, is there anyway we can kill Cooper and Palmer, who will testify against pa."

"The jail is a very secure building. The sheriff and deputy will have the help of private security guards, and these men are hard to kill. Even if we create a fire diversion, the sheriff or deputy may leave the jail to investigate, but the Rainbow Guards won't leave their post."

"How about poisoning Cooper and Palmer?"

"Ginny's Diner sends three meals at a time to the jail. If we poison two of them, there is a one in three chance that your pa gets a poisoned meal. Too risky."

"Any other alternatives?"

"Yes, there are two gunfighters in town that are very good with a rifle, especially the new center-fire Winchester 1876. If we put each of them on a roof or alley, we should be able to eliminate both Cooper and Palmer on their route to the courthouse. However, their price is $200 each, paid in advance."

"Hire them. Now the other issue is Plan B, how to revenge my pa. Clara's willingness to testify against Cooper and Palmer has led to pa's arrest. I want her and all her workers dead, and the buildings burned to the ground."

"Now here is the problem. You have a dozen cowhands, but that is what they are, cowhands. They are not willing to go on a murdering rampage. This kind of killing is not fighting 'for the brand.' Actually, it's a potential suicide mission if they mount a defense. This kind of mission requires professionals."

"Well in that case, I'll hire the ten-member Slater gang out of Kansas. If I have to pay their fee of $1,500, I'll include the total eradication of all five sheep farmers—starting with the Sullivan ranch."

***

The evening before the trial, Cal and Clara shared dinner at the hospital. The evening was spent in pleasant conversation. Cal was amazed how alert and well informed this lady was. Not to mention the fact that she was very pleasing to the eye with her atypical short blonde hair, bright blue eyes, nice curves and female attributes. Cal could talk with her and never have to look for words or subject matter. Cal had never experienced this type of female association.

Clara in return was working through her grief. She missed Levi and was totally lost as to how she would cope with the future. Yet, she found herself expressing her feelings to a total stranger. She eventually realized that it felt right, so she continued to share her innermost feelings. Talking to Cal was a natural process, and when he was not present in the room, she longed for his return. Clara knew she was smitten with Cal. Yet, she had no one to share the knowledge of this attraction.

With Rainbow Guards split between the hospital and jail, there were no further attacks during the night. In the morning, Cal went to see Sheriff Lovering regarding trial security.

Cal said, "The danger is to lose Cooper or Palmer before the trial starts. I recommend we escort one at a time and look out for sniper activity on route to the courthouse. So, if you agree, let's start with Cooper."

Half an hour before the trial, Wilson Whitehouse was escorted to the court and manacled to the defense table. They then escorted a manacled Cooper. Halfway to the courthouse, Max suddenly took off on a run behind the mercantile store. Without warning, a scream and animal growl erupted in an alley some three buildings away. Cal stepped up and saw Max attached to a man's thigh. This miscreant saw Cal and naturally lifted his pistol towards Cal. Cal produced an incredible fast draw and shot the attacker in the head.

After delivering Cooper at the courthouse, he was manacled to the prosecutor's table and kept under armed guard. Meanwhile, the security team was getting Palmer ready for his trip to the courthouse. Cal took a long barrel 10-gauge shotgun loaded with 00 buckshot. Sheriff Lovering reminded Cal that this was a special long-range hunting shotgun. Cal said, "that's just what I want for protection against a roof sniper."

The caravan started, and all seemed quiet till Max stopped and started growling, as he kept looking at the roof over the hotel. Cal immediately pulled back both hammers and waited. To everyone's surprise a head popped up with a rifle pointed at them. Cal lifted his shotgun, took quick aim, and fired both barrels. Cal was pushed back two steps from the recoil and the potential shooter disappeared from view through the heavy black noxious smoke. When Deputy Windman went to investigate, the roof attacker was dead with several pellet hits to the face, head and torso.

The trial finally began with Cal sitting with Clara. Also, in the spectator area were the other sheep farmers and their workers. The prosecutor presented two witnesses. The defense attorney tried to discredit Cooper and Palmer. Cooper insisted that Wilson Whitehouse had sent him to beat Clara Sullivan till she signed the bill of sale. Yet, he admitted that he hit her too hard and knocked her out before she could sign.

The same defense attorney tried to twist Palmer's testimony. It was Palmer who buttoned up the attorney when he said, "I come to a trial and admit to murder under the order of the defendant, and you try to tell me that I misunderstood the defendant's orders—I don't think so. I was clearly ordered to kill Levi Sullivan for a fee by Wilson Whitehouse."

While the jury was out, Cal said to the prosecutor, "why did you not include a charge for the murder of the other sheep farmer and some sheep workers?"

"Because we didn't have witnesses for those crimes. If we get a guilty verdict today, he will be sentenced for ordering an aggravated assault, and for ordering Levi's murder."

The jury took a long time but came back with a unanimous verdict of guilty on all counts. Judge Winter made a comment before passing sentence. "Mr. Whitehouse, I'm totally disgusted with you. You ordered a woman beaten into submission and ordered someone to kill a human being. Yet, you stand before me with a smug on your face. Sir, you are stupid. You had a huge productive ranch and now you have nothing. The maximum sentence I am allowed to hand you is ten years in the state penitentiary, without the chance for parole. At the age of 67, this may be a life sentence which is really what you deserve."

The courtroom went silent and the defense attorney added, "I object, we will appeal this conviction and this excessive sentence." The room eventually cleared, and Cal rented a buggy to bring Clara home. Two Rainbow Guards were left to assist Sheriff Lovering and the other eight followed Cal and Clara home.

Pedro and Elena had prepared the shearing shed as temporary housing for the Rainbow Guards. They added a table, chairs and beds. With a heating stove to make coffee, their meals would be served in the Rodriguez bunkhouse. Elena and her two daughters would be busy cooking for themselves, Cal, Clara, and eight men.

Cal set up a rotating schedule for daytime security. This included one man on the house porch, one in the barn hayloft, one on a knoll with pine trees some half mile from the homestead, and one parading on the grounds. The nighttime schedule included the other four men who would parade the homestead grounds and main house. Clara's bedroom window had been boarded up and with a full moon, the night crew had clear visibility.

Cal and Clara saw themselves enter the next stage of their business association and the development of their personal relationship.

***

CHAPTER 5—
The C-C Connected Ranch

Cal and Clara became comfortable and secure in the ranch house. Clara was still weak and needed assistance. She was beginning to walk outside, took short naps twice a day, and took her meals brought to the house by one of Elena's daughters. Cal did everything for her, he prepared her daily bath, he swept the house, cleaned the kitchen and kept coffee on the cookstove. Whatever Clara needed, Cal was there to provide without a complaint.

About a week after their arrival at the ranch, Clara made an announcement. "Ok Cal, I'm now recovered, and you are no longer needed as my caretaker. I will now cook our meals and take care of the house. But thank you for all you have done for me." Clara gave Cal an appreciative hug, but it lasted longer than expected. They found their faces nearly touching but they both separated before anyone would get uncomfortable.

The next day, Cal took a ride over Clara's 640 acres. He saw good grass lands, two very strong springs that generated a pond and a good stream, several large tracks of pine trees and a separate large stream going through the entire acreage. The soil was a rich loam to sandy loam with very few rocks.

After surveying Clara's land, he opened the neighbors gate and stepped on the next 640 acres. This section was now run by a widow, since her husband had been shot to death a month ago when he refused to sell to Whitehouse. Cal rode through the section which seemed very similar to Clara's land. The soil was the same but was barren of trees. There was plenty of water like Clara's land.

Several things were different. There were few sheep on the land. The land was a bit flatter and the grass was greener. There was evidence of active cultivation and irrigation, with new meadows approaching harvest time. There were sections of hay, oats and sugar beets. It appeared that the Gunters had already dedicated their land to growing crops and not raising sheep. Cal liked what he saw and decided to stop and speak to Mrs. Gunter.

Pulling in the yard he saw an open shed that held the agricultural implements. He saw a plow, harrow, seeder, hay cutter, hay loader, hay baler and other miscellaneous implements. The shed was open at both ends of each stall, allowing the implement to be drawn in by the horses.

The lambing and shearing sheds had been modified and joined to make a large crop storage shed. The large horse barn was new. The bunkhouse had an added cook shack and had evidence of families being housed.

Cal stepped up to the main house. "Hello, the house," an elderly woman opened the front door and asked what he wanted. "I'm Deputy US Marshal Cal Harnell and would like to talk to you about your ranch."

"Yes, I know who you are, please step down and join me for some lemonade."

Stepping on the porch, Cal expressed his

condolences for her loss. Mrs. Gunter thanked him and asked what brought him to her ranch.

"I rode through your land, you have few sheep, your buildings have been modified, and you have many cultivated acres ready to harvest. Plus, you have an extensive array of agricultural implements. Would you explain?"

"My departed husband had been working with Levi Sullivan in organizing the ten sheep farmers—four west and five east of the Whitehouse Ranch. The problem was that to increase the flock size, we need winter feed that was affordable. Getting winter feed from Denver was too expensive. So, my husband agreed to sell 500 sheep. With the $4,000 we bought agricultural equipment, fenced our section off with barbwire, and have now cultivated land for the past two years. This is our first harvest and we will supply the other sheep farms with all the winter feed necessary to increase their flock size and their income."

"What do you do for labor. Sheep herders are not the best of employees for handling a plow."

"Fortunately, we have many homesteaders

that have large families. Their sons are accustomed to handling horses and all the implements. The young single men want independence and are happy to work for a daily wage including room and board."

"Not to offend you but are you planning to continue your husband's work and run the farm?"

"Since my husband was killed, I've had a difficult time. My sisters in Ohio want me to sell, return to the home town, and join in their German restaurant enterprise. I have no children and so I'm seriously considering putting the farm on the market."

"Any predictions what your income might be this year?"

"With only 100 cultivated acres, my husband had predicted an income of $1,500 minus $500 for labor and expenses. The potential is to cultivate the entire 640 acres and become a commercial grower."

"Do you have any employees capable of running this enterprise?"

"Yes, there is a young man, Roger Crane,

who is a born leader and has much experience. He is planning to marry and as foreman, could live in the main house."

"What is your asking price?"

"I have $1,000 leftover from the sale of our sheep. The Whitehouse's offered us $5,000 but my husband refused and was killed because of that. For assets, we have $3,000 in equipment, the land is worth $1,000, and the buildings are worth another $1,000. The 200 pregnant ewes are worth $1,600. For a quick sale without real-estate commission, I would sell it for $5,500."

"I would be happy to purchase it. Here is a bank voucher for $500 to hold the sale, until we sign the final papers in ten days. If I change my mind, the deposit is yours. If you change your mind, the deposit comes back to me."

"We have a deal Deputy Harnell."

***

Meanwhile at the Sullivan Ranch, Clara was pacing the floors. Cal was going on a ride to check out the 640 acres. He should have been back in two hours max, yet it had been six hours and she was beyond worry, she was getting beside herself. Finally, she stepped on the porch to talk to one of the security guards. "Could I speak to the head of your team?"

"Yes, that would be me, Ma'am, my name is Clarence Simpson. How may I help you?"

"Cal left six hours ago for a two-hour ride over my land, he is late returning and I'm worried that something has happened. Could you spare a man to go look for him?"

"Yes, the night team is awake, and I will send a man to look for him."

An hour later, the security guard returned and reported to Clarence that Cal had not been found. Within minutes, a rider was seen coming down the access road. Clara's worries were resolved when she recognized the rider as Cal.

Cal stepped in the house and Clara rushed into his arms. She started crying and held on tightly. Cal gently placed his hands on her back and waited for Clara to stop crying. Clara finally said, "I know I am in mourning and I miss Levi, yet I can't control my emotions. I've grown comfortable with you and I thought I had lost you to one of Whitehouse's guns."

Cal added, "is 'comfortable' the right word, or is there more?" Clara nodded her head in agreement. It then happened, Cal and Clara were looking in each-other's eyes and both moved forward and kissed.

Both were working to increase the passion until they finally separated. Cal was first to speak.

"Clara, mark my words, I will always be here for you, I can't imagine ever being away from you. I have found a smart, alert and beautiful woman. I could talk with you for hours and never get bored. I also am having an issue controlling my emotions. I don't want to rush things, realizing you are still in mourning. Once we resolve this issue with Ray Whitehouse, we'll both be able to act more naturally. Now let's have a coffee and I have questions for you."

With the coffee ready, they were facing each other on the kitchen table. "I rode your land, you have 300 acres that are fenced with mesh sheep fence. That leaves 340 acres that is fenced with barbwire. You have good buildings to include a bunkhouse, horse barn, lambing and shearing sheds with storage. You have not started cultivating your land and you have not purchased agricultural equipment."

"That's correct, Levi's plans this year was to finish mesh fencing our flock in the southern 300 acres and securing our northern 340 acres against free range cattle. Cultivating our northern acres were plans for the future being developed with our neighbor, the Gunter's."

Cal was about to add his idea for expansion when he heard hoof beats and Clarence announcing two riders on the access road. Cal recognized the riders as Dan Whitehouse and foreman Stuart Wells. He stepped on the porch to greet the visitors.

"Hello Deputy, may we have a word with you and Mrs. Sullivan?"

"Certainly, step down and join us with coffee." With the coffee served, Cal asked, "what can we do for you." It was clear that Clara was not comfortable with these men in her house but went along with Cal for the moment.

Stuart started, "Ray Whitehouse is on the trail of vengeance. He wants to kill you and Mrs. Sullivan for his father's sentence. He wanted me and the twelve Rocking W Ranch cowhands to attack you to achieve his ends. I refused to be the hand of his revenge and the twelve cowhands agreed with me."

Dan adds, "to achieve his goal, he has arranged for a gang of hired guns. He has engaged the assistance of the Slater gang, lead by the infamous Winston Slater. This is a group of ten killers from the Nebraska area, who are expected to arrive today by train. What is worse, is that he will pay them $5,000 to eradicate you and then raid the other sheep farmers to your west. He feels that if he also can attack the other farmers, that they will cave in and sell their farms to him after you two are out of the way."

"Well that's a lot of important information. So, they could attack us as early as tonight or tomorrow morning! Tell me how you came onto this crucial intelligence?"

Dan responded, "the Plainsville telegraph operator is a friend of mine who also believes that the murderous activity of the Rocking W Ranch must come to an end. He shared this info with Sheriff Lovering who asked me to bring this information to you."

"Well, thank you and we will prepare our defense. Do you think Ray will also join this group of marauders?"

Stuart said, "I doubt it, he is a coward who lets others do his dirty work. He may watch at a distance with field glasses, but that's going to be as close as he gets."

As they were mounting their horses to leave, another rider was coming into the access road. The rider was identified as Sheriff Lovering.

Cal greeted the sheriff and asked him what brought him to the L-C Connected Ranch. "I need to be involved with an attack of this magnitude to our community. I plan to be here till the Whitehouse depredations are resolved, and the range war is over."

"We can always use another gun, especially a lawman. Go to the bunkhouse and Elena will set you up with a bunk for the night. In an hour we will hold a strategic meeting with the Rainbow guards."

***

The meeting was held in the shearing shed. Cal started the meeting by saying, "we are expecting a major attack from eleven professional killers, lead by Winston Slater. Some of you may not survive, so if any of you wish to step out of this fight, now is the time to say so and leave. I'm paying individual combat pay of $300 for those who participate."

When no one got up to leave, Clarence Simpson said, "we will stand by you to the end."

"Very good, here's my defense plan. I expect Slater will send four men through the open range to attack us from the north. He will have six men, plus himself, to attack us from the east. I would like two men hidden next to the bunkhouse and one man and Sheriff Lovering next to the horse barn to handle the northern attack. The attack to the house will be defended by a man on the barn hayloft, two next to the shearing shed, two next to the house front porch and one to the rear kitchen entrance. Clarence Simpson, your commander, will be the float to assist or replace any wounded guard. Your defensive position will be chosen by Clarence."

"I will be hidden behind a boulder on the access road and will pick off as many of the gang once they are on the property, some 400 yards away from me. There will be no shooting till I, Sheriff Lovering or Clarence warn the marauders to turn back or be killed. If they start shooting, before the warning, feel free to shoot back. Consider this gang as wanted 'dead or alive.' After the gang rides by me, I will follow them and provide fire-power from their rear. If any gang members put down their guns and raise their hands, don't shoot them down. They will be arrested after the shooting ends."

"Mrs. Sullivan, I want you to stand in the house archway between the kitchen and front room. If anyone attempts to enter through these two doors, you shoot them with your double barrel shotgun, before they can enter."

"Tonight, I expect this defense plan to be manned by half the men that rotate in three hours. I will spend the night at my post and Clarence will share a similar post behind the bunkhouse. A gunshot from either of us, will activate a full defense. Otherwise the full defense should be ready at predawn. I expect a full-frontal attack at that time."

Meanwhile at the Rocking W Ranch, Ray is meeting with the Slater gang. "In the early predawn, I expect you to attack the Sullivan ranch. Four men attack from the northern access first, then after the shooting starts, the rest of you do a direct attack through the access road, and immediately head for the main house where I expect the Marshal and Mrs. Sullivan will be located. I want everyone at the Sullivan Ranch killed, that includes women and children. After the massacre, head for the other sheep farms to the west. Ride through their homestead, burn one building and shoot anyone you see. Quickly move on to the next homestead and repeat your work. Any questions?"

Winston Slater says, "when do we get paid? The $5,000 is for my men, I charge $1,000."

"Here is $3,000. The other half is after the job is complete."

At the L-C Connected, Cal and Clara were making preparations for the night. Clara starts, "I am ready to do my part, no one will enter without getting a dose of buckshot. Are you sure you want to be out there tonight by yourself?"

"I'll be alright; besides we need an outlying warning system in case they decide on a nighttime raid. In addition, Clarence and I will already be at our posts for a predawn raid. Max will stay with you tonight and all day tomorrow. He will be your backup if you need help. Now, I need my Winchester 1876 and plenty of ammo. I will also bring a winter coat for the cold night. While I saddle my horse, would you prepare me some food and fresh water?"

When Cal came back to the house, Clara was waiting and handed him two bags of food and two canteens. "I'm including a snack and water for Clarence as well." As he took the bags and canteens, Clara moved up to Cal, planted a warm affectionate kiss, and said, "you come back to me, you hear!"

"I will, and don't hesitate, if someone opens those doors, stand your ground and shoot them!"

***

The night was quiet. By predawn, Cal heard hoofbeats that suddenly went quiet. About ten minutes later, gunshots were heard coming from the bunkhouse area. Amidst the sound of gun fire, the loud report of Clarence's Winchester 1876 was heard over the standard rifle fire of a Winchester 1873 and the pistol fire of a Colt. As soon as the gunfire started, Cal heard the hoofbeats again and finally saw the seven riders coming on the access road at full gallop with their pistols drawn.

Cal yelled out to stop, but the gang started shooting at him. The gunfire was useless at 400 yards. Cal then looked in his Malcolm 8X scope and fired. A rider was blown off the back of his horse. Cal had the time to shoot two more times and hit his target both times. By the third shot, Cal was running to his saddled horse to give pursuit and provide fire-power if needed.

As he was approaching the homestead yard, he saw a total gunfight in the process. The attacking group from the north was losing their efforts, two were dead, one wounded, and one had his hands up in surrender. Of the four to make it through his defense, all four made it to the front porch after shooting the two house-guards. Before they got off their horses, one outlaw was shot by a guard at the shearing shed. Three of the outlaws were hiding next to the porch shooting at the barn hayloft and shearing shed. One rider was seen jumping off his horse and heading for the front door with his pistol in his hand. One more outlaw was shot off the porch—leaving the last two men to enter the house.

Meanwhile in the house, Clara was standing firmly in the archway. Suddenly the front door opened, and Clara saw a man point his pistol at her. Clara pulled both triggers and the pistol carrying assailant was lifted off his feet and thrown over the porch onto the dirt. Clara quickly opened the shotgun to reload as another man appeared in the door-way and pushed in the screen door to enter. At that instant, Max growled and took a large bite out of the outlaw's abdomen. The man screamed to bloody hell as he readied himself to shoot Max. That instant Clara shot one barrel and hit the man in the chest. As the man went down, Max still held his hold till the final convulsions ceased. Clara last shot was the final shot heard. The attack had ended. The two gunfighters that had made it to the porch were killed by guards on the hayloft or at the shearing shed. The man who had received Clara's both barrels was Slater himself.

Sheriff Lovering was then preparing to bring the two surviving assailants back to jail to stand trial. The guards were then seen loading all the other marauders onto wagons for transport to the local undertaker, for identification and burial. Their pockets were checked, and each man had $250 plus loose change, which was considered part of their pay. Their pistols and rifles were gathered, and their saddlebags were checked for other valuables. When everything was collected, it consisted of: Eleven pistols and rifles, $3,397 in cash, fourteen boxes of 44-40 ammo, eleven horses with saddles and saddlebags. Everything was left to Cal and Mrs. Sullivan.

Clarence then brought his two wounded men to Plainsville by buckboard to see Doc Brewster. Their wounds were not fatal but needed cleansing and suturing. Sheriff Lovering followed with the two surviving gunfighters—one needed medical care. As he left, he told Cal to come to his office in two days to settle up on the bounty rewards.

***

After everyone left, Clara said, "is it finally over or are we to expect more repercussions from Ray Whitehouse?"

"What do you say we talk about that over breakfast of coffee, home-fries and eggs?" The cook would feed the Rainbow guards.

While Clara was busy preparing their meal, Cal gave Max a bowl of dog food and set it on the porch. He did not know what Ray was planning and Max was still needed on the porch to provide security. The coffee was first to be ready and they enjoyed the brew while the eggs and potatoes cooked.

During breakfast they started talking. Cal started, "I don't consider this a closure. Ray will not stop until both of us are dead, or he is dead. I doubt any of the two surviving men will implicate him before they go to the gallows. So, expect something from Ray in the near future."

"In that case, what do we do?"

"Retrospectively, Wilson did not get us with his Regulators and gunfighters, Ray did not get us with his army of marauders, and now I expect he will send an old buffalo hunter who does long range assassinations with a Sharps buffalo gun."

"How do we protect ourselves against something like that?"

"By thinking like an assassin. Where is the one place, we need to go that is outside the safety of this house?"

"The outside privy!"

"Correct. So, before we open the kitchen door and head out to do our business, we put out a dummy to see if the shooter will take a shot and be fooled. I will build a closet on the porch that we can remotely activate the door and move the dummy outside. You need to build a dummy out of some western pants and shirt stuffed with hay. Use a doll from Elena's kids for the face and place a big white cowboy hat on the dummy. If he takes a shot at the dummy, we will see the black smoke and I'll be able to return fire. It's a gamble but the alternative is to see the sun's reflection off a telescopic lens, and that's a matter of luck."

"Ok, start building the closet and I'll start sewing."

Cal got the buckboard ready and went to town to get some lumber. While in town, he stopped at the sheriff's office to inform them of his plans. He also hired Deputy Windman to check the train arrivals. He was to look for a man carrying a Sharps rifle or similar long-range rifles, and ride to Sullivan's ranch to tell Cal of the arrival.

Later at the Rocking W Ranch, Ray was meeting with an old buffalo hunter, Silas Morrow. Ray explained that he needed two people killed, a woman and a Deputy US Marshal. After all the details were given, Silas said, "I charge $1,000 for each and I want half the pay upfront. I will set myself up and watch for an entire day before I do the job, that way I always get my target."

"You have an open sight Sharps without a scope. Can you be accurate at long distances?"

"I set up at 400 yards and I can hit a coffee pot at that distance. As long as I can see the target, I'll hit it. I've never had a miss at that distance."

"Ok, here's $1,000 and see you when the job is done, that includes both of them dead."

With the dummy and closet finished and functional, a rider was coming on the access road. It was Deputy Windman, "you were right Cal. A scruffy looking dude arrived with a long barrel Sharps. He asked the ticket agent for directions to the Rocking W Ranch. He got on his horse and headed east." Cal paid him the $10 and Deputy Windman departed with a smile on his face.

"Well Clara, that means that the shooter will scout your land today and will likely spy on us all day tomorrow. I'm going to wait for him some 500 yards out in the tree-line. If I'm lucky, I will see the spot he chooses for his spying and shooting. I'll be back after he leaves."

Cal waited several hours when a rider arrived. He chose a spot near a large clump of pines with a view of the privy. He set his shooting sticks, sat down on the ground, aimed and dry fired his Sharps. After an hour of watching the ranch, he put everything away and rode off.

Back at the ranch, Clara asks, "did you find the shooter, and did he choose a shooting location?" "Yes, and he'll be 400 yards from the ranch house. Tomorrow, we need to establish a routine in the use of the privy. In the morning, I will be first to use the privy. After you take care of business, we will hold nature's call till

noon. That way, it will be an incentive for the shooter to take his shots in the morning or wait many hours for his next chance. We'll do the same between noon and dinner time."
Cal had no difficulty holding nature's call, but Clara was not happy waiting so long and used the chamber pot several times.

The second morning Cal was up first and started the wood stove to make coffee. After Clara was up, Cal spotted the shooter using his 8X Malcolm scope over his Win. 1876. Clara then pulled the rope opening the closet door, followed by remotely releasing the dummy to spring out of the closet. Within ten seconds, the dummy's head exploded in a cloud of white porcelain dust. Cal had the shooter's left shoulder in his telescopic sight and squeezed the trigger to fire. He saw the shooter violently roll to his left and was knocked flat on the ground. Cal rushed to get to his saddled horse and rode the 400 yards to find the shooter still unconscious. He then applied a pressure dressing to stop the bleeding and then threw some cold water in his face to awaken him."

The shooter sat up, saw a US Marshal holding a pistol on him and said, "well, it seems that I'm in a heap of trouble!"

"Yes sir, attempted murder of a US Marshal is a hanging offense."

"I want to make a deal, for a reduced prison sentence, I will implicate the man who ordered this hit."

"That can be arranged, but first let me bring you to Doc Brewster to have this wound looked at." Before he helped the shooter to his horse, Cal emptied his pockets and boots to be certain there were no knives or derringers. The last thing he did was to check his saddlebags. There he found $1159 which he pocketed.

Arriving in town, Cal sold the shooter's horse, saddle, saddlebags, Sharps rifle and scabbard to Willey's livery for $110. After seeing Doc Brewster, Cal brought Silas to jail and said to Sheriff Lovering, "the man is interested in a deal and is willing to name the person who ordered this execution attempt."

"Great, I'll take care of that. Now let's settle our finances. I gave you the vouchers for the two Regulators and the two gunfighters for $3,000. The two outlaws who tried to kill the trial witnesses came to $1,000. The Sheep Farmers Association reward was $2,000. The eleven Slater gang rewards came up to $13,000. That comes up to a total of $19,000."

"Ok, now for distributions. $4,000 goes to compensate widow Gunter, $4,000 goes to compensate widow Sullivan, $1,000 goes to the Rainbow Security Agency, $3,000 goes to the security guards as promised combat pay, and $3,000 goes to you, Sheriff."

"Why do I get $3,000?"

"Because you shot two members of the Slater gang and you get $1,000 for the use of your jail and honest services rendered, heh. And so, I'm left with $4,000. Before I go back to the ranch, I'll go to the bank to make the deposit and get some vouchers to distribute the funds. Also, let me know if the prosecutor and judge can make a deal and stop Ray from more depredations."

On his way to Clara's ranch, Cal pondered about extending Ray Whitehouse a peace offering. He could not find a solution since Ray wanted the sheep farmer's lands and revenge for his father's prison sentence.

When he arrived at the ranch, Clara was waiting for him on the front porch, standing next to Clarence Simpson. Once Cal stepped on the porch, Clara greeted him with a kiss that turned Clarence's head. Suddenly, they all heard a horse at full gallop coming down the access road. Cal recognized the rider as Deputy Sheriff Windman.

"What is the emergency, I just left the Sheriff Lovering's office?"

"I knew you had just left the bank, and I was trying to reach you before you got home. In any event, there will be a meeting in one hour between the Sheriff, prosecutor Nichols and Judge Winter. Your presence is requested."

"Well Clara, for the second time, our talk will have to wait again."

***

Sitting in the judge's chamber, the prosecutor proceeded. "Your honor. Two of the Slater gang and Silas Morrow were all hired by Ray Whitehouse to kill Deputy Marshal Harnell and Clara Sullivan. All three have signed their statements implicating Mr. Whitehouse. In return for their cooperation, should you agree, they are requesting a fifteen-year prison sentence without a trial."

"Assuming you are proposing this deal, I want to hear from both lawmen present."

Sheriff Lovering said, "by all means, this would put an end to the range war and save lives."

Cal added, "I agree, we need to resume peace in our community. I happen to know that Ray's brother, Dan, will offer the sheep farmers a fair settlement. The Marshal Service will support your decision."

"Very well, I will approve this deal, and in addition I am issuing an arrest warrant for Ray Whitehouse. I strongly recommend that both of you proceed to serve this warrant together—for your protection and the need of a witness."

Arriving at the Rocking W Ranch, Stuart Wells met them on the access road. When he realized the reason for their visit, he proceeded to town to get Dan to return to the ranch and take over operations.

Stepping down their horses, Ray walked out on the porch and said, "you two are not welcome here, so get out!"

The Sheriff said, "this is official business, you are under arrest for the attempted murder of Deputy Marshal Harnell and Clara Sullivan."

Ray face turned red and was exuding with anger. "I'm not going to prison."

"What are you going to do, draw against the both of us. That will make you a dead man, is it really worth it?"

Cal could see Ray start his draw in slow motion. As Ray's gun cleared leather, a shot ran out. Ray's gun went flying as well as his thumb. Ray screamed out as he was holding his mangled hand. Ray was covered in blood from a pumping artery. A tourniquet was applied, and after searching his pockets and boots for a knife or derringer, he was helped onto his horse to get sutured by Doc Brewster before being tossed in jail to await his trial.

As Cal was getting ready to leave, Sheriff Lovering asked Cal what his future plans were. Cal answered, "that all depends on Clara and I should know where things stand as soon as I get home. You'll be the first to know."

***

Arriving at the ranch, Cal went to see Clarence. He handed him a $1,000 voucher addressed to Eric Alderson of the Rainbow Agency for services rendered. He also gave him a $3,000 voucher for the ten men's combat pay. He thanked him and stated that they may meet again.

Walking into the parlor, he was greeted by Clara who held him in her arms and said, "is it finally over?"

"Yes, and for the third time let's have that talk. First, this is compensation for your loss from my victim's fund," as he hands her a bank voucher for $4,000. As Clara was about to speak, he added, "and this voucher of $4,000 is also for Mrs. Gunter for her loss. These victim's fund distributions are not negotiable."

"Now let's talk about our options. Clara you have two options. One is to sell this ranch to Dan Whitehouse for $5,000 and move into town. Buy a house and start an accounting business to take care of the books for cattle and sheep ranches. Your second option is to stay on the farm, fence in your entire 640 acres with web fence, start cultivating some areas to improve your pastures, increase your herd, hire more help and sell your water overflow to Dan Whitehouse. Plus, you build an addition to your ranch house for an accounting office."

"Now before you say anything let me give you my options. My first option is to leave, since my work is done here, and I need to move to my next assignment. The second option may be a shock to you. I have talked to Mrs. Gunter and I can purchase her acreage, farm implements and buildings for $5,500 and grow the 640 acres into a crop farm and grow hay, oats and sugar beets."

Clara looked at Cal and said, "there is no life for me unless you are in the picture. I'm in love with you, and that feeling will never go away. Both of the first options are not acceptable. We have to find a way to make both second options work."

Cal never hesitated, he took her hands in his and said, "lady, I have also fallen in love with you and cannot see a future without you. Will you marry me?"

"Yes," and it happened, Clara jumped into Cal's arms, kissing and their hands started roaming. Suddenly Cal scooped her up and carried her to the bedroom. That night, their passions peaked and were spent several times before morning. On awakening, Cal commented on the delight such a natural event could provide. Clara's answer was, "and it can be like this every day for the rest of our lives."

After another morning round of love making, they got up to prepare a replenishing breakfast. Sitting and facing each other at the kitchen table, they drank coffee while the bacon and potatoes were cooking. Cal asked Clara, "what do you want to do today?"

"I want to get married before you change your mind!"

"I would be so proud. But you are only weeks in your grieving year, what will the town 'holier than thou' say about that?"

"I don't care, those hypocrites don't know the power of love. Our marriage feels right, and if it feels right, it is."

"Ok, then let's tell Pedro and his wife and invite them to the wedding. Their son, Romano, can watch over the herd. The security team is heading to town and we'll invite them as well. On our way to town, we'll stop at Mrs. Gunter's house, to pay for her homestead, give her victim compensation voucher and bring her to town with us to sign over the deed at the land office, after attending our wedding."

"Breakfast first, then I change into my best dress and we are off."

"Can I watch?"

"No, it's bad luck to see the bride the morning of the wedding."

"Isn't it too late for that?"

"I won't tell if you won't!"

***

Packed for a short honeymoon in town, they stopped at the Gunter homestead. Mrs. Gunter greeted them and was surprised to find out they were going to town to get married. Cal hands her a bank voucher for $5,000, the balance due on the purchase price. She accepted the voucher with a thank you and a welcome to his new homestead. Cal then handed her the victim compensation fund of $4,000. When she learned its meaning she started to cry and shook her head in appreciation. When invited to the wedding and to the land office for a title transfer, she accepted. Now dressed in her Sunday best, she drove her buggy and followed them to town.

Arriving in town, Sheriff Lovering and Deputy Windman joined them at the courthouse. They filled out the necessary papers and Judge Winters performed the ceremony. Sheriff Lovering signed as witness. After the marriage, a reception was held at Bessie's Diner to include the guests and the security team. A large table was set up to accommodate seventeen people and lunch of meatloaf, mashed potatoes, fresh carrots, coffee, and bread pudding dessert was enjoyed by all.

After dinner, Mrs. Gunter joined the Harnell's at the land office.

The deed was transferred to Mr. and Mrs. Cal Harnell and Clara signed as Clara Harnell. Clara's deed was also transferred to the joint account. Property taxes were paid on both accounts and the Harnells headed to the National Bank where Cal had already transferred all his old accounts. As they entered, they were greeted by the bank president, Taylor Simpson.

"How may I help you?"

"We just got married, and we wish to transfer Clara Sullivan's account and my account into a joint account—Cal and Clara Harnell." Transferred were Clara's account of $500 and the $4,000 victim allowance and Cal's private account of $16,000 and his victim fund of $40,000. When Clara went to sign, she was shocked to see Cal's accounts. She hesitated, and the teller smiled to see a flummoxed lady. Cal just said, "it's OK Clara. Go ahead and sign, this is our money, not just my money, and the victim's fund will continue to be distributed to victims with either of our signatures." The paper work was completed, and new bank vouchers were given to the Harnells.

With all legalities completed, The Harnells headed to the Central Hotel for their honeymoon. On route, they stopped at the jeweler and bought wedding bands. Cal also saw Clara looking at the necklace display and he said, "which one do you like?" Clara said, "the necklace with a sapphire pendant and matching earrings is exquisite."

"Let's try it on." Once on Clara, he added, "this is you, and my gift to you on our wedding day."

"Oh Cal, this is too expensive at $800. Your love is all I want for a wedding present."

"You will have both for our lives."

***

For a week, the Harnells finally got to appreciate the town of Plainsville. They took the bridal suite with its own water closet and bathtub with hot water. Their nights were spent in wedded privacy. During the day they introduced themselves to the different merchants.

They started an account with Willey Blackwell at the livery, Ezra Woodard at the mercantile, Sam Burlaw at the saddle and harness shop, and George Small at Winslow Agricultural Implements. They introduced themselves to the Western Union telegraph operator, Bud Hall, and arranged to have telegrams delivered to their ranch headquarters at the original Sullivan ranch house.

They made business arrangements with the Railroad station manager, Glen Aronson, anticipating the need to freight their wool and buy more agricultural implements. They also made contact with the local freight company, owned by Silas McKnight, to transfer their new purchases directly to the ranch headquarters. During the week, they went back to the land office to change the farm brand to C—C Connected with subdivisions of Harnell Crops and Harnell Wool.

During the week they enjoyed their

breakfast and lunches at Bessie's Diner and got to know the waitresses and cooks. Their evening meal was taken in the Central Hotel dining room. Their daily afternoon entertainment was to ride out of town and target practice. Cal had bought Clara a Webley Bulldog pistol in 44 calliber. They practiced shooting at close range in self defense mode till Clara became proficient and comfortable with this handgun. She got use to carrying it in her reticule or in the dress pockets.

The last business arrangement was with the construction company owned by Murdock Williams. They arranged for the installation of a coal boiler, water closet with hot and cold water and a new windmill. The contract also included the house extension for Clara's office with a separate outside entrance and sign saying "Harnell Accounting." A second hay storage shed was ordered at the same time. Cal paid for the contract totaling $1,500 with a new bank voucher. Construction would begin in three days, and with two full teams of workers, would take two weeks to complete.

Having spent a great week in town and making some very important arrangements, the newlyweds were ready to return to their home and start a new life. How this life would meld with the Marshall Service was not yet clear to Cal or Clara. Before leaving town, Cal sent a telegram to Captain Ennis, it read:

TO: CAPTAIN ENNIS
MARSHALL SERVICE
DENVER, COLORADO

RANGE WAR RESOLVED STOP
HAVE JUST MARRIED STOP
STARTING A COMMERCIAL CROP ENTERPRISE STOP
HOW TO PROCEED WITH DEPUTY MARSHAL STATUS STOP
FROM: CAL HARNELL
C—C CONNECTED RANCH
PLAINSVILLE, COLORADO

***

CHAPTER 6—
The Julesburg Caper

The newlyweds arrived home with fresh vittles to replenish their larder. These included: bacon, fresh beef and chicken meat, fresh vegetables, coffee, milk, eggs, potatoes and dried apples. Cal brought the supplies in the kitchen for Clara to put away. He then brought their horses to the barn and took the last two stalls. He had forgotten that the ten horses confiscated from the Slater gang were housed in the barn. Cal made a mental note to keep three of the smaller horses at the sheep farm and to move the other seven larger horses to the crop farm for training to be harnessed for light field work. Seven of the saddles and saddlebags would be exchanged at Willey's Livery for new work harnesses.

For the rest of the day, they made the house their home. One spare bedroom was converted to a gun room to house the ten confiscated pistols and rifles from the Slater gang. Cal also added a large collection of previously confiscated guns. The other bedroom was kept as a guest bedroom or potential nursery.

With a wood fire in the main room fireplace and cookstove, he started the coal fired heating stove in the bedroom hallway. It became clear that with the addition of a coal fired boiler, it would lead to a coal adapter for the fireplace. This was commonly done in areas sparse in trees but abundant in coal.

By the end of the day, as Clara was preparing a chicken pot pie and both were drinking coffee, Cal brought up the subject of tomorrow's plans.

"I think we need to meet with Roger Crane at the crop farm and establish him as assistant manager/foreman. Upon our return we will have a similar meeting with Pedro. Plus, we need to arrange the transfer of seven work horses to the crop farm and bring the 200 pregnant ewes to your sheep farm."

"What 200 pregnant ewes?"

"Oh, those were included in the sale of the Gunter homestead."

"Wow, after the lambing that will increase my flock to 900 sheep."

"Yes, and both farms will need extra help."

After a wonderful dinner and cleaning the dishes, Cal and Clara sat on the sofa and started to read. Clara was reading a publication of Colorado taxes and exemptions, while Cal was reading a manual on growing feed crops on the Colorado eastern plains. Sitting next to each other while touching, both started to get bothered. This was a time when urges did not need to be suppressed. Kissing started and when hands started to roam, the house was closed down and the newlyweds headed for their bedroom.

The next morning, after a replenishing breakfast, the Harnells headed to the Gunter homestead. Arriving, they were greeted by Roger Crane. After introductions were made, they sat down in the Gunter office.

"Mrs. Gunter recommended you as a

potential manager/foreman. Can you go over your education and agricultural experience?"

"Certainly. I was raised in town and all through my ten years of schooling I worked on a homesteading farm as part time help. After graduation, my dad sent me to a 6-month agricultural school in Denver. There I learned about cultivation, fertilization, selecting seeds, planting and harvesting crops—especially hay, oats, alfalfa and sugar beets. It also included hands on experience with all the implements. After my graduation, Mr. Gunter hired me and for the past 18 months, I worked with him. We cultivated 150 acres and in one month we are ready to harvest 100 acres of hay, 30 acres of oats and 20 acres of sugar beets."

"Well you are certainly qualified. As you know I am still a Deputy US Marshal and may be gone for weeks at a time. Do you feel capable of being my assistant manager and foreman. I am planning to cultivate all 640 acres and harvesting all the acres. That will mean you will need to manage several fulltime employees and seasonal helpers."

"Yes sir. I can do it and welcome the opportunity. The problem will be housing since I am getting married in ten days to a widow with a five-year-old daughter."

"Let us make you this offer. A salary of $100 per month and the full use of this house. You buy your own food and have full use of the horse of your choice and the buggy if you need it. This is a seven day a week job. You will have purchasing power at all the town merchants and full hiring and firing rights. I will come daily to this office and use half of the desk and office, you have the other half. The office work will be kept from your private home and I will only use the outside entrance which Mr. Gunter was wise to construct."

"Oh, my goodness, that's a very generous offer. I would be proud to work for you and I will give you 110%. My wife-to-be will be in heaven knowing we will be living here. She is also willing to help if the need arises. Thank you."

"Great, welcome aboard. What do you need for this expansion?"

"We need one more plow and three heavy work horse teams. Especially if you wish us to cultivate some of your sheep pastures. We need to purchase some horse manure from nearby cattle ranches and we need a manure spreader. We need a phosphate spreader and some phosphate which you can get in town from the Crane Feed and Grain store (yes, my dad). And most of all we only have two full time workers and we'll need to have at least four more and a half dozen seasonal workers. That's for a start."

"OK, I will start an account at your dad's store for the phosphate, and order the plow, phosphate spreader, and manure spreader from George Small at Winslow AG. I will start looking for manure. Most important, I need to learn the business and will be asking you many questions. If you need more implements, order them and keep me informed. I will also hire the Murdock Williams construction company to enclose the entire 640 acres with barbwire. Don't forget to build the irrigation ditches needed to water the crops. Last, hire a good hostler and send your men to the sheep farm to pick up seven outlaw horses that will need harness training. I have also ordered the construction of a second crop storage shed. Otherwise see you at work soon. Remember when I'm here, I'm the owner. If I'm not here, you run the show."

"Very good. What do I quote workers for wages?"

"I will pay $1.40 per day for a 9-hour day. Breakfast is 6:30 to 7:30AM. Water/smoke break at 10.30 on site, lunch at the cook shack at noon for a half hour, water/smoke break at 3PM on site, and the work day ends at 5PM. Dinner at 6PM and the evenings are free to all workers. Room and board are included. You. take a day off, it's without pay. During the harvest season, I will pay extra wages for evening work when needed."

***

After lunch, they prepared for a meeting with Pedro and Elena. Clara took over the lead.

"Welcome. As you know, this farm will

be 100% sheep farming. We have hired the Murdock Williams company to enclose the entire 640 acres in web fencing. You and Romano need to go to the Gunter homestead, now the Harnell crop farm, to pick up 200 pregnant ewes. Over time, we will continue to increase our herd especially when the pastures are cultivated by Cal's workers."

Clara continues, "I would like you to become our head sheepherder and be responsible for the flock, lambing and shearing. I will be the general manager and we are building an office attached to our house."

"I would be honored to be your head sheepherder."

"In that case, your salary will be $100 per month, and we will build you your own home for your family. The bunkhouse/cook shack will be for the workers with their own cook. You and Romano will have your own horse to watch over the flock. Your only expense is your own food. If Elena wishes to be the worker's cook, she will be paid a salary. Romano will also be paid. Now we need to hire some workers with sheep herding, lambing and shearing experience. Any ideas where to get such workers?"

"First, let me thank you for such a generous salary and home. We are honored. As far as experienced workers, I have a widowed brother with two teen age sons working on a sheep farm some ten miles from here, with terrible working conditions. I am sure they will be glad to move and accept any income with room and board."

"Very good. After moving the ewes, please take a day and go see your brother. Take the wagon and bring them back. I will hire them, and we'll agree on a salary. Also, as we grow the flock, keep on lookout for new experienced workers."

"I will move the ewes tomorrow, and the next day I will get my brother and nephews. Thank you, senora."

***

The next morning, Cal was preparing to ride to town to take care of business, when a rider appeared on the access road. Cal recognized the rider as Dan Whitehouse.

"Good morning Dan, step down and come to the kitchen for some coffee. What brings you here today?"

"Time to come to an agreement with you, Clara, and your three neighbors to your west. I believe my family owes you an apology and some financial retribution."

"Well first of all there are only two neighbors to our west. Clara and I purchased the Gunter homestead."

"Let's start with your two western neighbors. How do I make things right with them?"

"Basically, they want peace. Also paying for their dead sheep at $8 a head will go a long way for good will. An apology will top the negotiations."

"I will take care of that personally. What about you and Clara. First, congratulations on your nuptials. How do I make things right with you?"

"By buying our hay or oats. We would sell you water rights to our stream that runs off our land and goes wasted by petering out in the open plains. Plus, we will buy or barter for your horse manure."

"Why on earth do you want my 50-year-old manure pile?"

"To fertilize my cultivated fields."

"Great, let's barter for hay. We'll settle on the values later. Now for my news. The two sheep farms to my east are for sale. The owners are too old to modernize their operations. I need the land and the water, so I will purchase both. That leaves me with a total of 200 young sheep of breed-able ages. I would sell them for $4 each or barter for more hay and oats."

Clara adds, "we'll take them and barter for your winter feed."

"Great, that only leaves two problems. The first is rolls of web fencing that I have no use for. As a peace offering, I will give them to you. The last issue is that we have some sheep workers out of work."

Clara again said, "send them to see Pedro, my foreman, for an interview. Shearing/freighting, lambing and breeding season will soon be on the way and we'll need extra help."

With the coffee pot empty and the meeting at an end, Dan rode west to meet with the two sheep herders. Cal picked up his list of businesses to visit and saw that Clara had added some household items to the list. Cal commented, "guess married life means that no one goes to town without asking if anyone needs anything, heh?"

Cal was able to take care of his errands and return home by dinner time. After dinner, a rider was heard arriving at the house. Cal looked out the window and recognized Captain Ennis tying his horse at the hitching rail.

Cal stepped outside with Clara, shook the Captain's hand and introduced his new bride. "Nice to meet you ma'am."

"Well, I never expected to see you here. I was expecting a telegram request for a visit to Denver."

"I wanted to see Plainsville, meet your wife, see your new homestead, and talk about the future. I have already met with Sheriff Lovering and he has told me how you resolved the range war. Nice job by the way."

Clara spoke up, "please come in, I have

apple pie and coffee for dessert and we can talk about the future."

After two pieces of pie, Captain Ennis started. "Colorado is such a large state that I have been authorized to establish six zones— north, central, and south for both east and west of the state. The Marshal in these six areas would be dormant and only activated when the need arose. I would like you to take control of the northeast section. While dormant, you can continue ranching. When activated, the state will pay you $30 a day plus you keep the confiscated horses, guns and bounty rewards if any. Are you interested?"

Clara interjected, "of course he is, and he will accept the position. My husband has shown that he is a master of his profession, and I whole heatedly support his lawman activities. I will pray for his safe return and I know he will always come back to me." Cal touched her hand and no words were needed to acknowledge Clara's support.

"Great, well let me tell you of an emergency assignment in nearby Julesburg. There is a gang lead by a notorious outlaw named Karl Mueller. He started this gang in Omaha and has been robbing banks in Lincoln, Grand Island, Kearney, and North Platte. Note that he has been heading west since Omaha."

"The gang is made up of seven toadies who perform all his evil wishes. In every town, they rob the bank just at closing, they kill all the lawmen and they only do their deed when nighttime has a moonless night. They follow the moon's cycles and use the three-day hiatus when the moon is between the waning and waxing crescent 1% moon. With the lawmen taken out of commission, and full darkness a short time away, no posse is ever organized till the morning when it's too late."

"Our intelligence reveals that they are on their way to Colorado and Julesburg is the likely next spot for their depredations. Should you accept the assignment, you have two days to get to Julesburg and put an end to this gang's activity before the three-day hiatus begins. The local sheriff, Jules Warner is requesting assistance, asap."

"I accept and will be on the train tomorrow morning. I will arrive in Julesburg by 10AM. That will give me time to work with Sheriff Warner to set up a safe defense."

"Keep in mind, this will require extensive gunfighting. All the gang's members have a wanted 'dead or alive' bounty and will not accept being arrested to hang."

"Acknowledged. Do you want to sleep here tonight?"

"No, thank you. I have a room reserved at the Central Hotel and will be on the 5AM train west to Denver. Good luck and do the job by staying safe. Send me a telegram when the caper is resolved. Nice to meet you ma'am." He doffed his hat to Clara as he departed.

***

That evening, Clara was especially active during their love making. Afterwards, she said, "how can you overpower all eight professional killers?"

"It requires the element of surprise and the use of the sheriff and his deputies. We may need to pick some sentries off before the robbery begins and all lawmen will have to shoot early with buckshot loaded shotguns. Basically, we need to put down the aggressors before their plan is placed into play."

"I hope you are bringing Max, I would feel better if you did." "Yes, Max has been on vacation since the Slater gang attack. Actually, he has been following the border collies and is becoming a good sheep dog. On this job, he will be my rear guard for any outlaw escaping the shootout."

***

In the morning, after a replenishing breakfast and a long affectionate good-bye kiss, Cal left with Boss and Max. As they arrived at the RR station, Cal paid for Boss to ride in the stock car. Max was considered a lawman's canine and was allowed in the passenger car. The sixty-mile trip took two hours. Capt. Ennis must have notified the sheriff because

Sheriff Warner was waiting on the platform to greet Cal and Max.

"I'm glad to finally meet the man who stopped the range war. Capt. Ennis gives you high praise, and that's good enough for me. Let's go to my office to talk."

As they entered the office, the sheriff introduced his deputies, Wayne Crenshaw and Paul Hurbert. "Our scouting reveals that the gang is already in town. They seem to be spread out between the three hotels and they frequent several saloons. The leader, Karl Mueller is a huge fella of over 250 pounds dressed in white with a tall white hat with a band of silver Conchos. His black gun belt and holster also have silver Conchos. His men have been identified by their wanted posters. They are all wanted for murder, robbery, kidnapping, and rape. It is a rough looking crew of scruffy and dirty outlaws."

Cal reviewed the wanted posters and committed each face to his photographic memory. After several cups of coffee and general talk about the layout of the town, Cal said, "I don't think they will hit the bank tonight. I will stay in the hotel tonight, and tomorrow I will scout the town. I will make arrangements with the bank and possibly some merchants. We will meet again tomorrow at 1PM to lay out our defense. Tomorrow, I will dress as regular city folk and if we meet do not acknowledge me."

"How do you know they are not robbing the bank tonight?"

"I will explain tomorrow at 1PM. Meanwhile, continue your usual activities. Just prepare by making sure your shotguns have plenty of #3 buckshot. Have a good day!"

Cal left Boss and Max at the livery and took a room in the Grand Hotel located close to the bank. After a full steak dinner at the nearby Susie's Diner, Cal took a bath and retired early.

The next morning after breakfast, Cal walked the town boardwalks looking like a gambler with a vest to hide his Bulldog pistol. There was an alley adjacent to the sheriff's office and a public barn behind the office to accommodate the merchant's horses. Entering the National Bank he noticed two tellers serving the public, the president's office was located to the right of the tellers, and the vault to the left of the tellers. The head teller had a desk behind the serving tellers and had his own serving window if needed. The vault door was closed and presumed locked.

Requesting a meeting with President Hobart, Cal introduced himself, "Hello sir, I'm Deputy US Marshall Cal Harnell. Tonight, I see you are closing late at 6PM. Anytime after 5PM you will be robbed. I will be here at 4:30PM to take over as a teller. Send a serving teller and the head teller home early. Tell the other teller to duck behind his counter when the shooting starts, and you keep your office door closed. I will shoot or arrest the robbers. Any questions?"

"I know who you are Marshall. We will give you a bank vest and visor to look the part, with a closed sign in your service window. Being open late, I will work as a teller to keep the customers moving out in a timely fashion. We'll be ready and thank you for your help."

Cal then proceeded to the gun shop

situated in front of the sheriff's office, and the barbershop adjacent to the alley next to the sheriff's office. After explanations were given, both merchants agreed to close their shop at 4:30PM and allow the sheriff or deputy to remain in the shops.

After lunch at Susie's Diner, Cal went to his meeting at 1PM. "Tonight, the robbery will occur. We are in a new moon cycle and for three nights, it will be a moonless night. Since the bank is closed Saturday and Sunday, the Mueller gang will be taking advantage of this moonless night to prevent a posse from tracking them. For the same reason, the actual event will occur between 5 and 6PM when darkness starts at 7PM. Now who is the best man with a rifle?"

"That will be Paul."

"Ok, assuming we are thinking like outlaws, here's the defense plan, based on the fact that I expect certain outlaw behavior. There will be three outlaws entering the bank with one man left to hold the reins of their horses. I will take care of those four and you three will be responsible for the other three shooters."

"Paul you will be hiding on the gun shop roof with a rifle, Wayne you will be hiding inside the gun shop with a shotgun, and Sheriff Warner you will be hiding in the barbershop with a shotgun. Those two buildings will close at 4:30PM and you need to be in place by that time. The three outlaws will likely be placed as such: one sitting on the boardwalk next to the gun shop, one on the barbershop roof or the hardware store next to the sheriff's office, and the third will come down the alley between the barber shop and the sheriff's office."

"As soon as the shooting starts in the bank, get ready. Things will happen quickly. Wayne, you open the door, step on the boardwalk, point your shotgun and yell, 'hands up,' The surprised outlaw will start to turn towards you, and you must shoot him immediately. The second outlaw waiting behind the sheriff's office will run down the alley to investigate. Sheriff get ready, as soon as the outlaw steps onto the boardwalk, take him out immediately. Don't let him turn toward you or you are dead. Paul keep looking for the roof shooter, take your hat off to keep a low profile, and as soon as he pops up behind the wall façade, you must act quickly. Take him out, you only get one chance, or you will be in a rifle gun fight. Any questions?"

"Why would they put a roof shooter?"

"To shoot any lawman who could escape the initial gun fight and start running toward the bank."

"What about the eighth man, Karl Mueller?"

"According to Capt. Ennis, he never gets involved with the shooting. He observes the activity from a safe spot on the escape route. Max will be in the vicinity. I have pointed Mueller out to him and if he tries to escape, Max will take care of him, and not gently."

"Assuming you are satisfied with the plan, I repeat, do not hesitate to shoot first. These killers won't give you a second chance."

***

That evening, Cal arrived at the bank on

time. With a white shirt, visor and the standard blue bank vest, Cal looked the part. The other two tellers were sent home, but President Hobart had to service one of the windows. A late bank closing always brought late customers. At 5:15PM Cal saw, through the bank bay window, four men arrive. Instead of tying the horse's reins to the hitching rail, they handed the reins to a man who stayed in the saddle. Three men stepped on the boardwalk and drew their pistols before they entered the bank.

Cal made a quick perusal of potential collateral damage. Both the president and the other teller were serving customers. As the robbers entered, one yelled out, "this is a robbery, give us your money or this woman dies," as he points his cocked pistol at the lady in front of President Hobart's window. Knowing the gang's history of frequently shooting one person at each bank robbery, Cal knew the "die was cast," and he had to respond accordingly and immediately.

Cal pulled his sawed-off shotgun hidden under a periodical and pointed it at the threatening outlaw, fired, and nearly decapitated him from a single shotgun blast. The lady at risk fainted and collapsed on the outlaw. Meanwhile, the other two turned their guns toward Cal and as they pulled their hammers, Cal shot between the two outlaws' heads and both dropped to the floor like a stone in water.

Cal ran around the bank counter, verified that all three outlaws were dead, asked President Hobart to assist the unconscious woman and ran outside to accost the outlaw holding onto the horse's reins.

"Put your hands up or you're dead." Two blocks west were heard: BANG........... BANG...............BANG/BANG. "Give up son or you will die, as the outlaw put his hands up and dropped the reins and his pistol to the ground. Cal handcuffed him to the hitching rail and then ran to the sheriff's office. As he arrived, all three outlaws were on the ground, dead. Cal then saw Mueller turn his horse and started galloping west of town. Cal yelled, "Max, attack."

Max was seen running west on the

boardwalk, then stepping onto a hitching rail, going airborne, and landing smack onto Karl Mueller. Mueller and Max slid off the horse as it reared from Max's attack. Max had Mueller's shooting arm/forearm in a tight grip and was trying to take a chunk of meat out, as Mueller screamed bloody murder. Cal and Sheriff Warner arrived on the scene and called Max off. Mueller kept pushing away from Max as he kept repeating, "keep that cur away from me."

With the event terminated, Cal did his usual routine. All eight outlaws, dead or alive, had their pockets and saddlebags checked out.

Cal gathered $742 in petty cash, which he pocketed. The outlaw's saddle bags had old clothing and useless items except for the 17 boxes of 44 caliber ammo. Mueller's saddlebags contained $6,000 in US Bank currency and $2,000 in US currency. These bank notes would be returned to the appropriate banks, but the US currency went into Cal's pockets. After the eight saddled horses were brought to the local livery, and the pistols/rifles were gathered, the local undertaker was called to remove the bodies. The undertaker's charge for burying six of the outlaws was $100 which Cal paid in cash.

The sheriff said to his deputies, "bring these two to jail, but before you lock them up, frisk them and remove their boots to look for a hidden derringer or knife. Mueller yells out, "I need a doctor for my dog bite."

Sheriff Warner answers, "no you don't, you would be lucky to die of blood poisoning before you hang."

President Hobart arrived at the scene as Cal asked, "how is the lady who passed out. Well as she lost consciousness, her intestinal and urinary track relaxed. She is still in the privy cleaning up. We have brought some warm water and soap. Plus, we went to the local mercantile to pick up a new dress and undies. I don't think that lady will ever be back in our bank." Cal was shaking his head and felt embarrassed. Yet, the sheriff was laughing out of control.

"Sheriff, what is so funny, this is sad humiliation for this victim."

"No, it's justice. This woman has been

critical of everyone in town and has been a rabble-rouser at the council meetings. This should knock her down a few pegs—and justly deserved."

"Today, I will send telegrams to the agencies that have posted the rewards. Let's meet in two days after the trial, so we can give you the Western Union vouchers."

"Ok, see you at the trial."

The next day, Cal went to the gun shop to sell eight Colt 1873 pistols with belt and holster. He was paid a total of $200 for the deal.

"Don't you also have outlaw rifles to sell?"

"No sir, those eight rifles will be crated at the RR yard and shipped to my home in Plainsville, to arm my employees."

He then went to see the hostler at the livery. The hostler had checked each horse, and said, "five of those horses are small, agile and will be ideal to handle cows. Three of the geldings, are very large and muscular, and would adapt to hauling or agricultural use in harnesses."

"Ok, make me a price for eight saddles, and those five small horses. I will be keeping the saddlebags and scabbards, which will also be crated with the rifles for home use."

"How about $40 per horse and $40 per saddle, for a total of $520."

"A bit low, but if you include new shoes for the three large geldings, free housing for Boss and the three geldings, we have a deal."

"Done, here's my hand to seal the deal. When are you leaving town, so I can get the geldings shod in time?"

"6AM, morning after the Mueller trial. I would appreciate it if the four horses would already be at the RR stock car corral by 5AM."

The trial started promptly at 9 o'clock. As the defendants entered the courtroom, Cal's jaw nearly dropped. The outlaw holding the horse's reins at the bank was not a guy, it was a woman with long brown hair and wearing a dress for effect. The prosecutor presented a riveting historical summary of Mueller's last four bank robberies in Nebraska. The defending attorney objected, but the judge allowed it. The prosecutor then described the events of the robbery without the defending attorney objecting. Marshal Harnell and Sheriff Warner did not need to testify. The defense attorney had no witnesses and the case went to the jury by 10 o'cock. In 15 minutes, the jury came back with a guilty verdict.

When it came to sentencing, District Judge Winters from Plainsville sentenced Mueller to hang at 8AM tomorrow. Before sentencing the other outlaw, the prosecutor requested to speak. "Your honor, my research reveals that the outlaw lady has never drawn her gun and only held the escaping horses. I request leniency and hope for a prison sentence." Judge Winters spoke, "ma'am, by law you are as guilty as Mueller, but I cannot sentence you to hang because of respect for your gender. Instead, I agree with the prosecutor and sentence you to the Colorado Woman's Prison for a term of ten years without parole. At 36 years of age, you will have the opportunity to restart your life. Court is adjourned."

Cal took the sheriff and his three deputies to Susie's for a fried chicken dinner. After lunch, they met is the sheriff's office for a financial settlement.

Sheriff Warner hands Cal seven individual $750 vouchers for the seven toadies and one $2,000 voucher for Karl Mueller. Cal in turn, takes three of the $750 vouchers and signs them over to the holding recipients. He then gives one to the sheriff and his two deputies. The three lawmen were obviously confused. Cal said, "you three men followed my directions and neutralize the three outlaws, and you deserve this compensation—not negotiable. In reality, I still end up with over $8,000 if you count the cash in the outlaw's pockets, the sale of pistols, horses, saddles, bounties of four toadies and Mueller. I will deposit half in my victim's account and half in my personal account via a bank transfer to my account in Plainsville."

That afternoon, he sent three telegrams. The first was to Capt. Ennis, informing him of the caper's end, the specifics and the total number of work days on account. The second and third was to Sheriff Lovering and to Clara, informing them of his arrival in the AM.

Arriving home, Sheriff Lovering was at the train platform. "Welcome back and we need to talk. Let's go to Bessie's Diner for breakfast and a chat, heh!"

With their order in and over coffee, Sheriff Lovering started, "In time, this problem will go away, but for now we have a cousin of Ray Whitehouse in town. He is a gunfighter and is here to kill you. He has beaten a saloon girl to an inch of her life and will be with Dr. Brewster for weeks. He also got into a gunfight with a gambler and killed him for cheating. All witnesses claim he drew on an unarmed man and threw a derringer on the floor before I arrived. I have several statements from the witnesses, but Paul and I are not capable of arresting a professional gunfighter."

"Say no more, I will find him and arrest him today, before I go home. Now let's eat our meal, heh."

Coming out of Bessie's, Cal had errands to run. He started by going to Doc Brewster's office. "Good morning Doc, I'm here to pay that saloon gal's bill, the one who got beat up by the gunfighter."

"She'll be here another ten days and I expect her bill will be $50."

Cal paid the bill, to Doc Brewster's surprise. Before Cal left, Doc Brewster said, "may I speak to you, privately?"

"Certainly, what can I do for you?"

"The missus and I are getting obsolete. We need new blood in this growing community. I have a young surgical senior resident at the University who wishes to practice in a medium size town. He can add surgery to perform life saving C-Sections, appendectomies, gall bladder and chest gun-shot wounds. His wife is trained in providing ether anesthesia instead of the dangerous chloroform. He knows how to use modern medical diagnostic and therapeutic equipment. I want him to come to town, but it's going to take money."

"I need to build a two-story hospital. The downstairs will have two examining rooms, an operating room, a delivery room and a large recovery room. The upstairs will house patient rooms, our apartment and an apartment for the new doc and his family."

"What is the cost and where is the money coming from?"

"The Williams Construction Company contract to build the hospital is for $11,000 and the diagnostic and surgical equipment comes up to $4,000. My wife and I are putting up $5,000 of our personal funds, and the council has an arrangement with the National Bank for a $7,000 loan. For the purpose of improving health care in our community, the council will pay the interest on the loan until the loan is paid off. So, we are short $3,000 to start the project."

"Say no more, here is a voucher for $4,000. That will give you funds to cover the new doctor's salary. If you need more, just ask."

"What interest rate and what kind of payment schedule?"

"Doc, this is a gift, not a loan. It comes from my victim's fund. We all know how much you help victims of crimes and you never charge them, heh!"

"Oh gracious, I didn't expect this, how do I thank you."

"Thanks, are not necessary, it is I and the council who thank you. I know that overruns on such a project are common. I will be here to cover them if necessary. So, get started. Build it, buy the equipment, and hire that senior surgical resident before someone else snatches him."

Cal spent the rest of the day looking for the gunfighter. He started at one end of town and hit all the bawdy houses and saloons. It was 4 o'clock when he walked into the last saloon/gambling house on Main Street, "The Ten of Diamonds." Cal walked to the bar, ordered a beer and asked the bartender if Ray Whitehouse's cousin was in the room. The bartender pointed to a man alone at a table playing solitaire. Cal left his beer on the counter, removed his hammer loop, and stepped to the man.

"If you are Ray Whitehouse's cousin, as a Deputy US Marshal, I am placing you under arrest for aggravated battery of a saloon gal and murder of an unarmed man. Stand and put your hands up."

The gunfighter looked up, dropped his cards on the table and slowly stood up, but kept his right hand over his pistol.

"Let me clarify a point. I am the man you were sent here to kill, but as you can see, I'm a US Deputy Marshal, and the attempted murder of a US Marshal is a hanging offense. You would be wise to surrender peaceably and take your chances in court with a good lawyer. With all the witnesses present, if you draw on me, I will shoot you in self- defense."

A moment passed, and Cal saw the gunfighter's pupils constrict. The gunfighter went for his gun, and as his barrel cleared the holster, a shot ran out. The saloon patrons assumed the gunfighter had accidentally discharged his pistol in the holster, but soon realized the gun smoke came from the Marshal's pistol. The gunfighter's gun fell back in the holster, as he saw the blood over the center of his chest. He then said, "you killed me," and collapsed over the card table.

As the sheriff arrived, the bartender explained the events, and Sheriff Lovering said, "unfortunately, this gunfighter is well known as one of the fastest gunslingers in Colorado. I hope this doesn't attract a slew of prima donna's who want to make a quick name for themselves."

"It is what it is, and it's the risk of this job. Maybe it's time I stop living by the gun, even if it's behind a badge, heh!"

***

Cal was happy to be on his way home, even if it was only four miles to the homestead, Cal found himself woolgathering about his future in the Marshal Service. He arrived home and as he was tying Boss to the hitching rail, Clara jumped into his arms and started kissing him. Cal pulled back to take a breath and said, "well lady, it appears you missed me, heh?"

Clara started crying and tried to speak but found herself blubbering. Eventually she said, "I can't function without you in my life. Yes, I missed you." "And I missed you as well." They kissed passionately. Cal picked her up, carried her into the house, and directly into their bedroom. Pedro had noticed Cal's arrival, but decided that the meeting with the senora could wait.

By 4 o'clock, Cal and Clara were in the kitchen having coffee while Clara was adding vegetables to the slow cooking pork roast. Clara said, "I was due for my monthly while you were gone, but it didn't happen. I blamed it on the stress of missing you, but this morning I lost my breakfast and now the smell of the pork roast is making me nauseated. Unless I'm mistaken, I think I'm pregnant."

"Wow that's big news and the best I'd ever hope for. A baby!"

"I have always wanted children, but it's a bit scary. There is a high mortality in child birth, especially the first delivery. Yet, I'm happy to be pregnant and willing to take the risk. While listening to Clara, Cal heard the carpenters building Pedro's house. Cal suddenly says to Clara to hold that thought and ran out to talk to the carpenters.

Within minutes, Cal came back with a smile on his face. "Darling I have some good news for you. Plainsville will have its own modern hospital in four months. Murdock Williams just confirmed the completion date. Doc Brewster is hiring a new surgeon who can perform general operations including a C-Section or complicated deliveries. You have nothing to worry about. This morning I gave Doc Brewster $4,000 out of my victim fund to make this project happen."

"I can't believe this is happening. What great news. I have read that careful prenatal care by a doctor is one of the best ways to avoid childbirth complications. As soon as this new doctor arrives, I will seek his advice."

"And the next time I go to town, I'll check with Doc Brewster as to when his new associate is expected to arrive. Now tell me what is new on the homestead, while I gaze at a beautiful mother to be."

"Pedro went to visit his brother and came back with him and his sons. They have been busy day and night with lambing. Pedro even hired two more workers from the closing sheep farms. One of these new workers has had training in a sheep veterinarian school and has been valuable with the lambing. So far, our lambing mortality is insignificant. The other worker is older and is returning to Italy after the lambing and shearing season. We also purchased those 200 sheep from the retiring farmers. Our permanent workers will be Pedro and son, his brother and two sons and this young worker with veterinary experience. Pedro also tells me that after the lambing season, we will have a population of +-1600 sheep. Our wool harvest and meat sales will be significant."

"What are you offering the workers for wages?"

"Unlike crop workers where a daily wage is ideal, the sheep worker is accustomed to long hours of watching the flock at night against predators. So, I offered each worker, except Pedro, $40 a month with room and board, and paid time for going to church on Sunday. Elena and the two girls have taken over the worker meals. I am paying her $15 a month and each girl $5 a month for helping their mom. The Rodriguez are very happy with their new home being built, plus they also get their meals at the cook shack and will be able to bring their meals in their new home when completed."

"With the larger flock, are we having problem with predators?"

"Yes, we need to leave a man riding all night on horseback. With a shotgun he has killed several wolves, coyotes, and foxes."

"I will help them with the predator problem. I'll train them to use a rifle, and to quickly reload a double barrel shotgun. I'll also bait the predators to help reduce their numbers."

"Now what about you. Are you getting involved with the daily operations?"

"As far as the lambing, I'm in charge of the nursery. Premature or weak lambs are kept in the birthing shed with their mothers. I take care of the babies. I milk the mothers and bottle feed the newborns that need help. I enjoy it and the mortality is way down. When it comes to shearing, I will help with the wool cleaning, sorting and baling. I did this last year and enjoyed the work. I also do the books for both farms."

After dinner, Clara went over the books with Cal. First, they went over the payroll, livestock purchases, miscellaneous lambing tools and general medical supplies. Basically, she described how the business accounting was laid out. She then showed him the books on the crop business. Roger had been busy with many expenditures and new employees. Cal decided to bring these books to the crop farm to discuss the numbers with Roger.

The next morning, Cal arrived at the crop farm with ten 1873 rifles and thirty boxes of 44 ammo.

"What in heck, are we going to war?"

"No, but I expect anyone working for me to be proficient and accurate at a 100-yard target. If there is another sheep/cattle range war, I want us to be capable of defending ourselves."

"Oh, and before I forget, any worker who wishes to go to church on Sunday does not get their pay docked. It is included in their room and board—got it?"

"Yes, boss. That's a nice touch, if I may say so."

"Now fill me in, I can't wait to hear what the outside activity is all about."

"The day after you left, McKnight Freighting showed up with implements from Winslow Ag. It included a reverse furrow plow, a phosphate spreader, manure spreader and a baler."

"How is that possible, I had just ordered them, but I didn't order a second baler."

"The first three implements had been ordered by Mr. Gunter and never picked up. This note came with the baler."

Cal read the note, "A gift to the man who gave my two mothers an easy week and refused payment. Enjoy? Wayne Swanson."

So, with the extra plow and the harvest about to begin, Cal started interviewing after placing a notice on the Woodard Mercantile bulletin board. He quickly found out that there are many homesteaders with sons that are ready to leave home. They are experienced with ag implements and eager to earn an independent wage and living situation. Many plan to share there income with their families and meet with them every Sunday morning for church services. After the interviews, Cal hired four permanent field workers, four seasonal harvest workers and a hostler.

"By the way, tomorrow is the last day cultivating land, and we start mowing tomorrow as well."

"I'll be here to watch both. I'll be watching the harvest and be willing to help out if you need extra help. I need to learn the process and sometimes working is a great way to shorten the learning curve."

"How about horse power. Where do we stand."

"Willey Blackwell has been a good source of draft work horses. He brought a matched team of Percheron's with new harnesses from Sam Burlaw. Three days later, he arrived with a matched team of Belgian's with new Burlaw harnesses. He is now trying to locate the third team I requested. We need draft horses to handle the plows and the geldings can handled the other implements."

"How is the geldings' harness training coming along?"

"Our new hostler is a Cheyenne Indian. He is an older man by the name of 'Gentle Wind.' The other workers call him 'Win.' The man is a genius with horses. He has already broken all those outlaw horses to harnesses. He has a grunting language that I swear the horses understand. It's an art to watch him harness horses to implements. The only problem is that he has an elderly wife and they live in a native tepee behind the barn. The wife works all day in the barn with the horses and your barn is like new—she cleans it. They both speak English and seem very happy here. I'd like to continue the arrangement."

"Sounds great. Now where did you get all these miscellaneous tools to include" manure forks, hay forks, baler twine, round shovels, heavy weight oil, grease and more?"

"We have a new hardware store in town. Ezra Woodard's son has opened a true hardware store that has allowed Ezra to expand his clothing line and double the grocery section. The new hardware is called 'Forks and Wrenches.' You need to open an account like you did with other merchants."

"Now what about you. Did you get married?"

"Yes, and we've moved into the Gunter house. Susie brings the workers fresh water with a tank in the light wagon. During their water break at 10:30 and 3, she oils and greases the implements. During the harvest she will likely be doing the finish raking. When Susie works, our daughter is taken care of by Win's wife. They all get along nicely."

"Didn't you go on a honeymoon?"

"We put that off till after the harvest. This job is very important to us and we want to make it work. This the busy time and we need to be present."

"What a great start. My only request is for you to give Win's wife a salary, as the hostler's helper. Now, let's go over Clara's books."

Roger looked at the ledger, checked every entry, and said, "wow, what a nice professional accounting. The bottom line is that I spent a lot of money when you were gone. Did I overdo it?"

"Certainly not, I think that this is great

management, on your part, when I'm gone. Today, I'm going to town to pay some bills and I'll be back in the morning."

"While at the hardware store, pick up some mechanical tools: wrenches, pliers, screwdrivers etc. We need some, especially when we start the harvest with implements more sophisticated than a plow or harrows."

Cal stopped at the house for lunch with Clara.

"How are you doing with this 'morning sickness' thing?"

"I talked with Elena and she gave me some soda crackers. I'm to take them on awakening, before getting up. I'll try that tomorrow."

"Anything new with the lambing?

"Yes, we lost three ewes and their lambs to a pack of wolves last night."

"I'll be solving that problem tonight. Ask Pedro to bring the dead animals to the gulley on the northern fence line—where he has left carcasses before. Tell him not to bury them but to eviscerate them to increase the smell of dead flesh. I'll be back before dinner."

While in town, he visited every merchant to pay any outstanding bills. He also met Ezra's son, Lyle, at the "Forks and Wrenches," and set up that account. There he bought several tool boxes of wrenches, pliers, screwdrivers and too many tools to mention.

Once done with accounts, he went into the new gun shop in town.

"Hello, my name is Cal Harnell and I need some shotguns."

"Welcome to the Culligan Gun Shop, my name is Ken. I believe you know my father in Julesburg. He told me how you stopped the Mueller gang. Pleased to meet you. Now, how many shotguns do you want?"

"Six new double-barrel 12 gauge shotguns, twelve boxes of #3 Buckshot, six boxes of OO Buckshot, six adjustable web belts/shell holders, ten boxes of 44-40 ammo and six shotgun scabbards."

"Wow are you in luck, I just received ten new Remington's with exterior cocking hammers. These are a new production for $39 each. If that does it, your bill comes up to

$326—$234 for the shotguns, $18 for the 18 boxes of shells, $9 for the six web belts, the six scabbards are $10 each for $60, and $5 for the ten boxes of 44-40 ammo. The six gun-cleaning kits are included. Thank you for your business Mr. Harnell."

After loading the armament in the buggy, Cal headed home. On arrival, he went to his gun room with two of the shotguns/scabbards and came out with four 1873 rifles/scabbards. He went directly to the cook shack where the workers were finishing dinner.

"I have here four shotguns, ammo and carrying belts as well as four 1873 rifles with ammo. I will show you how to do a quick reload with the shotguns and Pedro will train you in the proper use of the shotgun and rifle. I expect you all to be able to fend off a wolf pack attack, and I also expect you to be able to hit a coyote at 100 yards. Practice ammo is free. No one goes to the pastures, day or night, without a rifle and a shotgun on your horse. If there are no questions, let me show you how to do a quick shotgun reload, and then you can practice after dinner."

During dinner, Cal explained how he was going to go wolf hunting at the sheep cemetery. He would be on site at dark. During their dessert, they heard a rider coming in. Cal got up and recognized the rider, Bud Hall, the telegraph operator.

"What are you doing here, you have young messengers for this job."

"Everyone was home, and this came in on closing. Not a big deal for me to travel four miles to your spread. It's marked urgent." Cal gave Bud a dollar tip which impressed the telegrapher. Cal read"

FROM: CAPT. ENNIS MARSHAL SERVICE DENVER, COLORADO	TO: MARSHAL HARNELL PLAINSVILLE, COLORADO

FOUR MEN OF THE RAINBOW AGENCY HAVE DISAPPEARED STOP

OWNER E. ALDERSON IS REQUESTING YOUR ASSISTANCE STOP

PROCEED IMMEDIATELY TO BOULDER OFFICE ON FIRST TRAIN TOMORROW. STOP

Cal looked at Clara, "I will take care of this emergency and stop to see Capt. Ennis on my way home. Time for decisions. I want more freedom to get involved with the business of crop farming and living the family life. For now, I cannot leave without decreasing the wolf population. I'm going hunting and will be at the train station at 5AM for the first train west. Tell Roger to stay on schedule and start the harvest. Changes will be coming soon."

***

CHAPTER 7—
The Rainbow Affair

Cal got to the sheep cemetery/gully at nightfall. Pedro had done a good job at eviscerating the carcasses. Cal knew that with this kill, the pack would be around to eat their game. Cal set up on a fallen tree overlooking the gulley. Both long double-barrel shotguns were loaded with #3 Buckshot and his snub nose shotgun was also loaded with the same buckshot. His web belt/holder was full, with ten shells in place. As a backup, his rifle was loaded with fifteen rounds and placed on the tree next to the shotguns. Except for his holstered Colt, all guns had their hammers at full cock. With the help of a full moon, Cal was ready. Boss was tethered 100 yards away to a pine tree, but Max was at his side.

Things were quiet for several hours but around midnight, the wind came up and Cal was standing downwind. With no warning, an eerie single howling was heard that startled Cal out of a peaceful place. Cal looked around, and upwind, two bright eyes appeared. A second howl brought on a cacophony of several howls. Within a minute, Cal saw a bunch of eyes followed by the full pack of wolves. The pack went straight for the gulley. Cal took aim and let go two shots with the first shotgun, picked up the second and fired both barrels. The result was a pile of down wolves.

Cal quickly reloaded and as he looked up, the remainder of the pack was charging him. A black alpha male was in charge of what appeared a half dozen full size wolves. Cal started shooting and went thru all three shotguns before the pack and the alpha male were down. He then walked around and dispatched any wounded animal. Before he left the cemetery, all the carcasses were rolled into the gully after Cal eviscerated them. Whether these carcasses would be a deterrent to predators or more food was not clear to Cal. What was clear, the sheep and the herders were a lot safer with this pack eliminated.

Cal got home around 2AM and was able to get a few hours of deep sleep. He awoke at 4 o'clock to the smell of bacon. Carla was up, eating soda crackers, with a big smile and kiss waiting for Cal. She had already packed Cal's two saddlebags under the understanding that if Cal needed a packhorse, he would rent one. After the departing kiss, Cal headed off Clara's usual line by saying, "I know, you'll come back to me. Afterall, we have a child to raise, heh."

Cal boarded the westerly train and slept all four hours to Denver. There, he changed trains and headed south to Boulder. After proper directions, he rode to the Rainbow Agency, accompanied by Max. Cal entered the small office and was greeted by the owner, Eric Alderson.

"Good morning, how may I help you."

"My name is Cal Harnell, Deputy US Marshal, sent to you by Capt. Ennis."

"Thank God you're here and thank you for coming so quickly."

"This is the first time the Captain sends me on a job without visiting with him first.

He actually sent me here with a short telegram stating that some of your men had disappeared, so please fill me in."

"That was an intentionally misleading telegram. Actually, four of my men have defected and gone rogue."

"Are any of these men part of the team I hired a month ago?"

"No, they are newly hired men that saw the shiny dime instead of the dirty dollar. It is presumed that they kidnapped a twelve-year-old boy and a four-year-old girl."

"How much do they want for ransom?"

"Money is not the issue. These are the kids of a popular politician who is the swing vote on an important tax bill for the oil producers. The kidnappers are holding the kids, till dad votes against the bill in two weeks."

"You presume to know the kidnappers by name, and I bet they abducted the kids without wearing a face mask. So, that means we have two weeks to save these kids before they disappear forever."

"Assuming the kidnappers are your old

employees, they must have been paid a very large amount of money to do this dirty deal. Any idea who could afford this kind of expense.?"

"Any of three major oil barons in the county could afford the fee, which would be a drop in the bucket, compared to the new tax they would have to pay on each barrel of crude oil."

"Ok, I'm in, but why just me? Why not the full US Marshal Service?"

"Because of the sensitive nature of stealing votes or bills, the kid's dad wants them rescued without any official lawman involved. We want you to do the job without your badge and with a false name. As of today, you are Joe Caruthers from Arizona."

"So be it, any leads where I can start?"

"Yes, there have been four fractionated telegrams from two communities. By adding the four telegrams, we were able to piece up their demand. The two locations come from: Wheelman, some seven miles west of Boulder, and Nederlan, some ten miles west of Wheelman. That's seventeen miles of tough mountainous country, to find these outlaws before two weeks."

"How often do they contact the father and which of these two towns was last to send a telegram?"

"The politician insists on a telegram every three days and some proof the kids are still alive. The last one included the girl's favorite doll's name. The last communication came from Nederlan, so we expect the next telegram to come from Wheelman in two days."

"Very good, tell dad I'll get his kids back as Joe Caruthers, before the scheduled vote. What is the politicians name?"

"Samuel Whitcomb."

***

Cal quickly made his way to Wheelman. He put up Boss in the local livery close to the telegraph office. Took a room in the nearby hotel and went to lunch in the local diner. After lunch, he went to see the telegrapher.

"Hello, my name is Joe Caruthers and I have a proposition for you as he places a $20 Double Eagle on the counter. You have sent two fractionated telegrams recently from an unknown resident, sent to a political office in Boulder."

"Yes, and by law I've reported them to the sheriff."

As Cal slips a second Double Eagle on the counter, "the next time this happens, would you step to the window and wave your visor?"

"Certainly, since this is not against company rules, I will be glad to do this, as he scoops up the two Double Eagles."

The day went by and several people came to send telegrams: the sheriff, some court officials, several ladies and even a cattle rancher surrounded by his cowhands. Cal was sitting on the boardwalk across the office and stayed there till the office closed.

The next morning, Cal was in the diner and saw a man arrive before the office opened. As the telegrapher arrived, the man entered with a paper in his hand. Cal was immediately suspicious, stepped outside and walked to the man's horse and poured a liquid on the horse's right rear hoof and lower leg. Cal went back to the boardwalk and waited. The man came out and climbed in the saddle on the horse's left side and showed no signs of detecting the powerful cedar scent.

After the customer clearly left town, the telegrapher came to the window and waved his visor. Cal walked across the street and went in the telegraph office. On the counter was a paper that said, To Samuel Whitcomb, Capital Building, Boulder Co. The text said, 'the boy's horse is named, Spitfire.'

Cal went to the hotel to pay his bill and get his firearms and saddlebags. After a full breakfast, he then picked up Boss. Now that an hour had gone by, he felt certain that the outlaw would not pick up a dust cloud or even see a rider following. Before departing, he opened the scent bottle and had Max take a good whiff. "Ok, Max follow and find this dude's camp."

Several miles later, Max was on the scent until they came upon a large stream. Max was doing some extra searching because the scent had washed off the horse's hoof and leg. Cal started following the tracks the old fashion way. Eventually, the scent came back as the horse's leg dried up, and Max took over again.

Suddenly, Max came to an abrupt stop. His ears perked up as if he could hear men talking. Cal stepped down, tethered Boss on a long rope to a branch, picked up his Win. 76 and his sawed-off shotgun. They made their way along the tracks till Cal could hear them talking some 150 yards away. He then spotted the camp with his 8X Malcolm scope and saw the four men standing around the campfire. Fortunately, the two kids were about 50 yards away, playing in their tent. Cal made the decision to immediately and decisively act, unknown to him that he was being watched by a hunting party of Cheyenne Indians.

Cal took careful aim and sent a 45 caliber bullet the distance and hit his target as one of the outlaws was lifted off the ground and hurled backwards. Cal then stepped sideways away from the black smoke cloud and heard several bullets hit the nearby trees. He reloaded and took his second shot. The outlaw was twisted sideways and collapsed. The shooting continued and Cal realized that these men were good with their rifles since the rounds were getting closer with every shot.

Cal got behind a large boulder but was now closer to the camp by 50 yards. During changing positions, the remaining two outlaws also sought protection behind large pines. What Cal didn't know was that one outlaw had run towards Cal and was now only 50 yards away. Cal looked thru his scope and finally picked up one outlaw behind a tree. He took aim and pulled the trigger. The outlaw was thrown backwards and collapsed.

Cal then made a fatal mistake. While levering another round, he accidentally lifted his body above the boulder when a shot ran out and hit Cal in his left shoulder. Cal was knocked down to the ground. He immediately pulled out his sawed-off shotgun, from the holster on his back, and covered it with leaves. He waited and suddenly the outlaw was standing over him. The outlaw angrily said, "you bastard, you killed three of my friends but you are now going to hell." As the outlaw pointed his rifle at him, Cal lifted his shotgun out of the leaves, and pulled both triggers. The outlaw went airborne and landed on his head. Cal then realized that he was losing consciousness as everything went black, and then there was nothing.

In time, Cal opened his eyes to see a half dozen Indians standing over him. One was holding a steel cervical collar on a chain, the restraints he would use on a captured outlaw. The leader of the Indians said, "you not Iron Man, I know Iron Man. His name is Wain." Cal realized the Indian was referring to Wayne Swanson of Silver Circle. Cal said, "Wayne is my friend," as the lights went out again.

***

The next time Cal woke up, he found himself in a teepee. A squaw had shaken him to awaken. She offered him a liquid and said, "drink, will make you stronger." Cal noticed that his wound had been sewn with fine sinew and appeared not to be infected. Over the day, he became stronger and was able to talk with the Cheyenne chief. The chief came over to palaver. "I'm Chief Blue Sky."

"Thank you, Chief Blue Sky. You saved my life. Where are the children?"

"They are playing Indian games and your dog is with them."

"I need a favor. I will give you a note to give to the sheriff in Wheelman that explains who the children are, who I am and who to contact to return the children to their parents. The sheriff will also send word to my woman and my boss. In return, I will go with you to the Indian Trading Post and exchange the outlaw horses and saddles for food—for your people. I will also give you the outlaw rifles and many boxes of ammo."

"In your tongue, you say, 'what a deal'? Give note and the children will be returned today. When you are stronger, we go to the Trading Post. One day you will tell real 'Iron Man' of our meeting."

Three days later, a 2-mile trip was taken to the Trading Post. "Sir, I'm Deputy US Marshall and I have five outlaw horses with saddles and one packhorse with pack saddle. What is your offer?"

The trader looked at the horses and said $250 in cash or $400 in store credit."

"We'll take store credit. Start adding up and tell me when I get to $400. We'll take ten live beef from your corral. 30 pounds of flour, 30 pounds of potatoes, 5 pounds of coffee, 5 pounds of sugar, 10 pounds of salt, and…….."

"Stop, you have $5 left."

"Add $5 worth of hard candy for the kids. Now make it fair, I know we're not up to $400 of store credit."

"Ok, I'll add 100 ears of corn since I have a surplus. That's it."

"Deal, but we select our own beef."

"Ok. I'll start collecting the dry goods as you choose the beef."

When they arrived at camp, Cal noticed that Chief Blue Sky was proud to enter with the gifts for his tribe. Later he said, "I did not know you wore the same gold star that Wain had when he rescued his woman."

A week later, Cal was strong enough to

get on Boss and return to Boulder. His first stop was at the Rainbow Agency. Eric greeted him and invited him into his office. "Everyone appreciates what you did. You were not aware, but Samuel Whitcomb is a very wealthy real-estate developer. He has left this envelope for you."

Cal opens the envelope and reads the note: *I will forever be grateful for returning my children and saving the integrity of the congressional system. Accept this check/bank voucher as a token of my gratitude. Plus, if you ever need a favor, feel free to call upon me. Respectfully—Samuel Whitcomb.*

Cal looks at the voucher and sees the amount of $5,000.

"Now let's talk business. I'm getting along in years and I want to retire. My business is for sale. I have 20 certified guards, and we serve 20 businesses. I have 20 more men that serve outlying communities, just like the men you hired a month ago. The selling price is $8,000 and it includes this office and the apartment upstairs."

"Thanks for the offer, and the price is fair. However, I already have two businesses in

Plainsville and a loving pregnant wife to go with them. Besides, it's time I stop living by the gun. Thanks again but goodbye."

Cal took the train to Denver to have an important meeting with Capt. Ennis of the Marshal Service. As the train approached the station platform, he noticed a lovely woman searching the passenger car windows. Cal knew he was coming home.

Cal stepped on the platform and sneaked up to the woman who was frantically searching for someone. Cal softly said, "I told you I would come back to you." Clara was stunned and started crying. Cal held her, and words were not needed.

During lunch, Cal had to relive the entire story, including his brush with death. Clara never even hinted at the dangers of the job. She listened and expressed thanks that Cal was Ok. On their way to see Capt. Ennis, Clara just held Cal's hand in silence. When it was time to enter the Captain's office, Cal brought Clara into the office with him.

"This was a simple take down, yet I managed

to get shot by the last standing outlaw. I think I'm getting complacent or preoccupied, and either puts me off my game. I need till next spring without assignments, so I can decide what to do with my life. By then, our first born will arrive, the businesses will stabilize, and I should be able to give you my decision regarding the Marshal Service."

"This is a wise move, certainly better than handing me your resignation. So, you'll be on leave without pay, and we will meet again in the spring. In case you forgot, you are eligible for disability pay equal to three months of full service pay."

"Ok, send the funds to my victim account. See you next spring."

***

Cal and Clara took the train at 2 o'clock and were in Plainsville by 6 o'clock. Pedro was waiting with the buggy at the train station. Their ride home was a continuous story of everything that happened on the sheep farm since Cal left. Pedro and Clara were alternating and going from one issue to another, for the entire four-mile slow trip to home.

Pedro started, "the workers have been practicing their rifles every evening. The have become proficient and accurate at 100 yards. They have killed many fox and coyotes. No wolves have been seen."

Clara added, "the lambing and shearing seasons have been out of sync this year. The Gunter flock was at full gestation, and Pedro didn't think we had time to shear them before lambing. So, we performed an emergency crutching instead."

"What on earth is crutching?"

"It's a procedure where the pregnant ewes had the wool sheared from the anal, vulva and udders. This provided cleanliness throughout the birthing process."

"Ok, so why was the process out of sync?"

Pedro took over the explanation, "by the time we finished lambing the Gunter flock, our own flock began lambing. Fortunately, our flock of pregnant ewes had already been crutched. With lambing now completed we are ready to start shearing. Next fall, we will delay the breeding season, so we can shear in March and lambing in April—the proper sequence to keep the wool clean."

Clara took over. "Now the freighting issue. We are expecting a robust wool harvest. We don't have enough storage. Pedro worked out a great deal with the railroad and the McKnight freighting company. I'll let Pedro explain."

"Well Senor, it's very simple. We don't have storage or heavy wagons to haul the wool. The railroad will build a large dry storage shed to receive wool anytime and ship it to the Denver mills on their schedules. In addition, Mr. McKnight has made us an offer we could not refuse. They would haul all our wool as long as the bales were no larger than 3X3X3 feet. That comes to a 200-pound bale and our press can handle that size and compress it."

"I assume the savings is in the purchase of the wagons!"

Clara adds, "no, the freight bill equals the expenses of a team and wagon over a three-year period. The big savings is manpower.

During shearing, we don't have time to start hauling wool to the railroad."

Pedro continues, "there are two more issues we want to tell you. Mr. Williams will finish my house in three days, then he will not be available for four months to build the new hospital. Fortunately, we have a new construction company started by a local man named Milton Blakely. They are eager to get work, and I have hired them to fence off separate pastures to promote a grazing rotation. They will also build us paddocks to help selecting animals. This includes two more stalls for treating or crutching the animals."

Clara closes by saying, "the last item is a major expenditure and I feel we need your approval. We feel we need some winter protection for our lambs. We would like a large roofed shed with west/north walls. It would also include a special feeding bin that doesn't allow hay to fall on the sheep's wool. We would reserve it's use for lactating ewes, their lambs, and any sickly animal. This would keep our winter kill down. Mr. Blakely has given us a bid of $700 for its combined construction. What do you think."

"First of all, you never need my approval. But in this case, it appears this is a wise business decision. Our profits will reflect its construction, and our flock will be healthier as well. If Mr. Blakely is available, let's get started."

Arriving home, Cal made it to the main parlor, sat down on the sofa, and appeared exhausted. "I'm still very weak from all the blood loss. If it wasn't for the Cheyenne Indians, I would have died out there and may never have been found."

"It's not healthy for you to dwell on that. We are lucky that you are here and 'now' is what we need to concentrate ourselves on. Tomorrow, go see Roger and observe the harvesting operation. I did two days ago, and I thought he needed more help than he had. See what you think, heh!"

After a dinner consisting of a beef pot-roast, potatoes and carrots, they enjoyed some intimacy with Clara in the lead. The next morning, after a replenishing breakfast, Cal had Pedro saddle Boss, and headed to the crop farm. On arriving, things appeared excessively busy. Roger came over to welcome him back. Cal said, "I want to see the harvesting sequence from beginning to the end. I'll be back later, I'm heading to the field to start with mowing."

Mowing was a slow process, but with two men and two teams, the fields were getting cleanly mowed. Cal moved on and saw a teddering machine in action to promote drying. The next step was using a side rake to make rows for pickup. The side rake was making perfect rows. Following the side rake, the loader was rolling over the rows and the hay was falling into the attached wagon. One man was stacking the hay to fill the wagon. When the wagon was full, it was exchanged for an empty one. The loaded wagon was heading to the baler in the homestead yard. Riding back, Cal saw a lone worker, riding the finish rake, and making perfect straight rows. He realized it was Susie Crane.

As he was following the loaded hay wagon

back to the baler, he computed that eight men were needed to get hay to the baler: two on mowers, one on the tedder, one on the side rake, one on the loader, one stacking hay, one transferring wagons and Susie on the finish rake. He thought, *who was bringing water and servicing the machinery with oil and grease?* The answer was obvious when he saw an Indian woman and a young blonde white girl hauling a water tank and barrels of oil/grease. Again thinking, *this is a well-organized system and it appears it's adequately staffed.*

Arriving at the homestead yard, things were not busy, they were hectic. The horse was easily walking on his own to turn the cam that operated the baler plunger. Everyone else were running like fools. The man feeding the baler hopper was also helping to unload the hay wagon, <u>he needed a helper</u>. The man tying the baler twine was hopping like a monkey from one side of the baler to the other, <u>he needed a helper.</u> Seeing the second baler in similar operation, the same helpers were needed. The bales from both balers were loaded on a wagon and another man was stacking them. When the wagon left to get unloaded, a second wagon appeared in its place with its own stacker. Suddenly, the horse was stopped, and both balers stopped for water break.

"Roger, you have a perfect operation in the field. Each worker works independently, and each job is well staffed. The baling stage is understaffed, and you need five extra workers."

"Yes, we started with this number of workers for one baler, but because the hay was building up, we started the second baler. I can't afford to stop to go to town to get more workers until tonight."

"Not a problem, I'm heading to town and will come back with five more workers. Where do I find them?"

"Here is my list of eight names. I interviewed them and anyone would work well and fit in with the other workers. You'll find them in the saloons or sitting on the boardwalk. Find one and the others will be quickly located. Why five, we need only four?"

"No, you need to manage things, and only

fill-in when absolutely necessary. That way, if someone is sick, your operation doesn't come to a standstill. Do you need anything in town?"

"Yes, my season's order of baler twine was scheduled to arrive today, pick it up and save on the freighting fee."

Cal went directly to town in the light duty wagon. On arriving, he went to see George at the Winslow Ag. The twine had arrived and would be loaded while he was hunting down some workers. Cal was on his way to the nearest saloon when he walked by two hardy men sitting on the boardwalk. "Any of you men on this list?"

One man looks at the list and says, "I'm Steve Merchant and this is Red Swift."

"Great, you men still want a job with Roger Crane?"

"Yes sir, and the other men on that list are in the Ace of Spades saloon."

"Get your gear and horse, if you don't have a horse, my wagon is being loaded a Winslow Ag. We'll be leaving as soon as I find three more workers."

Cal arrived with a full wagon load of twine

and two workers. The other three had their own horses. Win took the three horses to the barn and all five workers were sent to the bunkhouse to settle in. Lunch would be ready in a half hour and Roger would show them their job after lunch. All five were told they would get a full day's pay for today.

Cal had lunch with Roger. It was clear to Roger that Cal was still weak and needed to go home and take a nap. "As soon as you are stronger, come back for a business meeting."

"I'll be back tomorrow, to watch the process first hand. I may not have the stamina to physically help out, but I have the ability to watch and possibly come out with some beneficial ideas."

As Cal was leaving to return home, he never noticed a man some 800 yards away, using a 50X Binoculars on a tripod with leather shields to prevent the sun's reflection. The observer was of German descent and went by the name, Hans Mueller.

***

CHAPTER 8—A New Life

Cal spent the next three days recovering at home. Clara was feeding him some iron rich foods to replenish his blood loss. After several walks and rides on Boss, Cal finally felt able to return to the crop farm and observe the activities.

Arriving before breakfast, Cal hoped to meet with Roger in the office. Susie greeted Cal and said, "Roger wants your opinion, so have a seat at your desk, and I'll be back from the cook shack with a pot of coffee and some egg sandwiches."

"Thank you, ma'am, well Roger where are you up to with the harvest?"

"Harvesting ten acres a day, we'll be done with the 100 acres of cultivated hay in three days. Then we have three or four days to harvest the 30 acres of alfalfa. After that we harvest as much of the remaining 500 acres of wild and natural uncultivated hay—by choosing the most fertile and productive areas. The last to be harvested is the 20 acres of sugar beets—they need the cold weather to harden and preserve."

"Are you going to have enough storage for all these crops?"

"The original storage shed will be 100% full with cultivated hay and alfalfa. The new shed will also fill up with oats, straw, wild hay and sugarbeets."

"Nice to hear you'll have enough room for the entire harvest. But that doesn't allow growth in the future."

"No, and that's one of the issues we need to resolve."

"I'll work on that one, what else.

"We are still experimenting and studying the balance and need between cattle ranchers and sheep farmers. Cattle ranchers want wild hay and oats for horses and cultivated or wild hay for cattle winter feed. Sheep farmers want alfalfa, cultivated hay, oats and sugarbeets. When we cultivate your sheep pastures, we will plant short grasses with less stems such as orchard grass, forbs (broad leaf plants), and clover."

"So far, this goes along with my reading. How do you feed sugar- beets to sheep?"

"We add the entire plant to a grinder that converts it to shreds. We then add water and let the shreds soak for an hour. The swollen shreds are then fed, and because they are hydrated, the sugarbeets do not cause bloating."

"Ok, I'm going to town to see if I can resolve the storage issue."

Arriving in town, Cal picked up Silas McKnight and went to see the railroad manager, Winthrop Casings.

"Mr. Casings, I have a storage issue. Pedro tells me you are planning to build a storage shed for our wool."

"Unfortunately, the railroad executives have nixed that idea as too expensive and requiring the double handling of the wool. Instead we have built a siderail to hold enclosed box cars to receive your wool bales. We could also receive your bales of hay if you arrange some companies to buy your crops. Actually, the box cars are already on the siderail, ready to receive your hay"

Mr. McKnight added, "because the

railroad has killed our freighting business, we are on the verge of closing our operation. If we were to get your freighting business, we would widen our wagons to hold an efficient load of hay bales. We could be ready with modified wagons as early as tomorrow morning. Your costs would be cheaper than you could achieve with your workers. Time is money."

"Gentlemen, we have a deal. Tomorrow, I'll go to Denver and find some buyers for cultivated hay, wild hay, alfalfa, straw and oats." Before heading home with the good news, Cal sent a telegram to Wayne Swanson, requesting a list of potential buyers that he wasn't able to supply—thereby not competing against him.

After he informed Roger, he reviewed everything with Clara. During dinner a messenger arrived with a telegram from Wayne Swanson. It included a list of seven retail feed stores and forage distributors in need. It also included the going prices for all the products they had for sale. Cal packed and planned to be on the train to Denver by morning.

After productive negotiations, Cal returned

home with three signed contracts. The prices offered were comparable with Wayne's, and it included all the crops they were growing. The biggest demand was for cultivated hay and alfalfa.

Returning to Roger with the good news, he found McKnight was leaving his modified hay wagons on site. They were already hauling the full wagons and replacing them with the empty ones."

Roger added, "This is working out, we are saving on unloading the wagons and stacking the bales in the storage sheds. I wonder if some of the nearby sheep and cattle ranchers would also leave some wagons and start hauling them, at a discount since we save on delivery time and labor."

"That's a good idea." Looking at the wall map, Cal said. "I'll visit every rancher within five miles of our operation. I'll even consider bartering bales for manure, which we'll need."

"Great, but since we'll be hauling manure with our manure spreaders, only barter with ranchers within two or three miles."

"I guess, that means we need to order a

second and third manure spreader, heh. I'll order them the next time I'm in town."

"Yes, and later we need to talk about how fast you want to cultivate our land—which will require more implements."

"Agree, see you after my visits with the ranchers."

Cal started west of the crop farm. Being three miles to town, he also visited every rancher two miles west of town. The reception was enthusiastic. Having done the math with Clara, Cal was able to give these ranchers a discounted rate if they came to pick up their hay from the storage shed, and the best discount was if they loaded their wagons from the baling site—either by leaving their wagons on site or loading them as the bales came off the baler.

The ranchers to the east of the homestead were given the same offer. The first cattle rancher was Dan Whitehouse's Rocking W Ranch. Cal wanted the fifty-year old pile of horse manure since this was only two miles to the crop enterprise. Clara had computed the value of a load of manure equal to so many 50-pound bales of wild, cultivated hay, straw, or bags of oats. Dan was all in and signed a contract.

Deals were also made with sheep and cattle ranches east of the Rocking W Ranch. All deals were made on a first come, first serve basis because of the limited supply of products their first year. All customers were guaranteed that with a major expansion of cultivated hay, there would not be any limits next year. This guarantee would allow ranchers to expand their herd next year.

Cal returned home and had a detailed meeting with Clara. That evening, they prepared sale prices to give to the customers arriving to pick up their product. Each load was to be invoiced according to the number and type of bales purchased. It was clear that while the harvest continued, Clara would need to be at the office to prepare the invoices for each load.

The next morning, Clara joined Cal and went to meet with Roger. Clara would explain the price schedules, and then a planning meeting would follow.

Meanwhile, Hans Mueller was watching the

ranch house with his high-powered binoculars. He reasoned that this was a poor site to stalk and perform the killing shot. There was no cover and he decided to go back to the crop farm where he could hide in the tree line and get a good 600-yard shot at his target. Besides, Harnell spent more time at the other farm, and it provided more opportunity for his revenge.

***

The financial portion of the meeting was quickly over, especially when Roger realized that Clara would spend the remainder of the harvest season, to work in the office and invoice every load. He then said, "Next year you will have a little one to care for and coming here to process the orders would be very inconvenient. May I make you an offer. My widowed mother-in-law will be moving in with Susie and me. Susie is also with child and due in the spring. My mother in law has worked for the Plainsville tax office for years and would be capable of running this office."

"Yes, that would be wonderful, and I would provide her all the training she would need."

"Now let's move on with the future. As it stands, 100% of our crops will sell this year. Just keep enough forage for our sheep's winter feed. Our expansion potential can be unlimited. I have four buyers eager to sign a contract over the three we already have for this year. As the saying goes, 'time to make hay is when the sun shines, heh.'"

"This sounds good, what do you propose?"

"To increase our production, I propose that we buy two more plows and one more disc/finish harrows. That would include three teams of draft horses and the workers needed to make this happen."

"I agree 100%. Our seasonal workers are capable and willing to become year-round employees. I'll get the Blakely Construction Co. to expand the barn and the implement shed."

"At the end of the harvest, our workers won't need to haul our product since Mr. McKnight will take care of that."

"That means that our cultivation team can

start work at harvest's end. We would continue work till the earth freezes. Let's hope for a late or mild winter. That way we will plan on an early planting of hay, a mid season planting of sugarbeets and alfalfa, and a late planting of oats."

Clara interjects, "don't forget, we need to cultivate 40 acres of pastures for the sheep. By planting time, I will arrange for new fencing to divide the acreage into individual sections for grazing rotation."

"With these changes, how soon can we start cultivating?"

"I will hire a new batch of seasonal workers to finish the harvest. That will allow me to do a major reassignment of jobs. The only two workers I must keep are the experienced men on mowers."

"Great, go ahead and hire more help, do your reassignments and training, and I bet I can get the new implements and draft work horses here before you're ready. I'll even go see Mr. Blakely to arrange for the barn and implement shed extensions."

Roger adds with a smile, "I accept the challenge."

That afternoon, Cal and Clara went to town using the light duty wagon (buckboard). Arriving, they each went their own way. Clara took the buckboard and went to the hardware store, to meet Eric Woodard at the Forks and Wrenches. She picked up some new shearing shears and a roll of specialty wrap for wool bales. She then went to Woodard's Mercantile and picked up fresh meat and vegetables to supply the cook shack and their own larder. Ezra was also holding some packages for the Rodriguez family from Sears. After loading the order and Pedro's packages, Clara rode on to catch up with Cal.

Meanwhile, Cal had been busy running his errands. First stop, the Blakely Construction Co. where he designed a barn extension with room to store bales of hay, and heated winter living quarters for Win and his wife. Next on the list was George Small at the Winslow Ag store. He ordered the implements with a rush surcharge. Next door he went to see Willey's livery and the Burlaw harness shop, to order three more matched pairs of work horses, Belgians and Percherons. Mr. Burlaw would build harnesses to fit each animal. His last stop was the National Bank. Cal made a cash withdrawal to meet the payroll of both farms. He also made a deposit from the income of selling sheep. Pedro had culled the flock after the shearing of non-reproducing animals. These sheep were sold to meat buyers.

With their business completed, they were headed home when Sheriff Lovering intercepted them. "Cal, we have a problem. Would you stop at Doc Brewster's office and speak to his new associate, Doctor Walter Woodard?"

Approaching the office, they noticed the new hospital under construction. Meeting the new doctor, Cal said, "Hello we are the Harnells. With the name of Woodard, are you related to Ezra and Eric?"

"Yes, Ezra is my uncle and Eric is my cousin. They were instrumental in attracting us to this community. How may I help you?"

"Sheriff Lovering said that you have a problem."

"He must be talking about Martina Bramhold. This lady has been severely beaten by her husband, Harvey. She has been in a coma for two weeks and is finally awake with some severe residual. It will take weeks for her to walk again. The problem is that the sheriff cannot do much to help her. If he arrests her husband, he will spend five days in jail and then probably beat his wife as punishment for filing a complaint against him."

"I see, well here is a $100 voucher to pay for her care, as long as it takes to get her back on her feet. I will take care of any balance in charges. Meanwhile, may I spend a few minutes with Mrs. Bramhold before I leave?"

After spending time with the patient, Cal said, "I will go see her husband today, and I assure you the problem will be resolved." On their way out of the office, Clara met the doctor's wife and set up an appointment with the doctor for prenatal care.

Talking outside, Cal asked Clara if she could return home by herself. He would borrow a horse from Willey and head out directly east to the Bramhold ranch. Clara assured him she could make the short trip to home. Before leaving Clara asked him how the meeting went with Mrs. Bramhold. "She wants to be free of her husband, so I gave her a voucher for $4,000 from my victim's fund and guaranteed she would be granted a legal divorce. I'll be back by dinner time, after my visit with the husband."

While riding to Bramhold's ranch, Cal thought of what his wife had said. She spent ten years being his indentured slave. She cooked his meals, did the laundry, fed the horses, saddled his horse, mucked the stalls, cleaned house, did the shopping, satisfied his violent sexual demands, and couldn't get any money to buy clothes or to feed herself properly. In return he would beat her regularly, especially after going to town to drink and go whoring. By the time Cal got to his destination, he was determined to bring this man to his knees.

Meanwhile, Clara was almost home when she came to a bend in the road, and a rider was standing in the middle of the road. Clara's horse reared and nearly rolled over the buckboard. Settling the horse down, Clara screams out, "what the hell is wrong with you, you nearly caused a collision. Please move out of the way."

The rider moved closer to Clara's horse and said, "heh little lady, what do you say we step in the bushes and have some fun?"

Clara grabs her reticule, pulls out her Bulldog pistol and says, "I'm not going to repeat my request, either get out of the way, or I'll shoot you out of the saddle."

The rider gave Clara a furtive look, stepped aside and said, "we'll meet again someday, soon!"

Clara took a careful description of the man, and continued home.

Arriving at the Bramhold ranch house, he stepped on the porch and knocked loudly on the door. As the door opened, Harvey Bramhold said, "who are you and what do you want?"

"I'm an acquaintance of your wife and I'm here to talk to you."

"You mean that dumb Mexican peasant. Did she die or something?"

"No, shall we step into your office?"

"If you insist, follow me."

Entering the office, Cal picked up a stone name plate on the desk, and as Harvey sat in his chair, Cal hit him in the mouth with the stone plate. A half dozen teeth went flying and Harvey was stunned beyond belief. "Now I'm going to give you a fraction of the beating you gave your wife."

Cal sent three round punches to his face, took his pistol and smashed it on his left knee cap, and then put a solid punch to his testicles. The man was roaring and screaming when a cowhand appeared at the office door.

Cal looked at the cowhand and said, "I'm giving this animal a fraction of the abuse he gave his wife. If you want a piece of this, walk thru the door." The cowhand turned around and left.

Harvey was still holding his privates and vomiting all over his desk. Cal then said, you are one stupid mean drunk. Instead of treating Martina like a real wife, you treated her like an animal. You are one fat pig while your wife looks like she is starving." Harvey seemed like he wasn't paying attention, so Cal took his trigger finger and bent it back to the top of his hand. Harvey's eyeballs popped open and he started squealing. "The next time you're not paying attention, another finger will go backwards."

Harvey muttered, "What's it going to take for you to go away and never ever be seen again."

"A financial settlement and a divorce for your wife. Martina has been your servant for ten years. At a dollar a day, that comes up to $3,650. Plus, a $1,000 as compensation for the beatings. Tomorrow, you will go to the courthouse, sign the divorce papers and leave a voucher for $4,650 with the judge."

"Never happen in this lifetime. Go to hell."

Cal never hesitated, he straddled Harvey in his chair, opened his mouth and shove an awl in one of his rotten molars. Harvey's pupils dilated, his limbs went stiff and then started violently shaking. As he started screaming, he wet himself. Cal pulled the awl back and asked if they had a deal.

"I'm going to kill you for this."

"Guess no deal yet." The awl went back

in but in another molar. The result was the same, but this time Cal was tweaking the awl in multiple directions. Harvey was responding with every tweak with a violent jerking and groaning. Eventually, he looked like he was about to pass out, as his bowels loosened and he messed himself. "Do we have a deal, or do we try another tooth?"

"Yes, but I never want to see your face again. I'll be in to see Doc Brewster to fix my knee and then will do the paperwork at the courthouse. What about my trigger finger?" Cal unceremoniously grabbed the finger and slowly bent it back in shape—associated with another prolonged final scream from Harvey.

When Cal arrived at the livery, Pedro was waiting with Boss. The Sheriff was also present to find out what to expect. Cal told him, "Harvey will be in tomorrow to sign the divorce papers and leave a hefty compensation check of $4,650."

"How did you manage such a settlement?"

"Best if you don't ask and don't know!"

Along with Pedro, they headed home.

Pedro took some time to bring up the subject of the senorita's encounter with a troublesome man. As Cal entered the house, he went up to Clara and took her in his arms. "Are you ok, is the baby ok?"

"Yes, thanks to the Webley Bulldog pistol. I was able to handle the situation."

"From now on, anytime you need to go to town, you will do so with me or one of the workers armed with a shotgun. Promise?"

"I'm not worried about me, but because of the baby, I'll gladly agree with your request."

"Great, now describe what this dude looked like."

"He was a huge man approaching 250 pounds and likely be six and a half feet tall. He had a mean look, wore all black and was covered with silver Conchos on his hat band, belt and holster. He even rode a large black stallion. His pistol had a white pearl handle, and he had a scoped Sharps in his scabbard. And last, his boot tips were also silver."

"Wow, are you sure you don't have ancestors that were lawmen? That's a perfect description.

Tomorrow, I'll pay a visit to the saloons and hotels. Maybe I'll be lucky and find him."

"Just be careful, he looked like a cowardly back shooter."

The next afternoon, as promised, Cal went to town to find and confront this man. First, he stopped to discuss the issue with Sheriff Lovering. "I can't believe any man has the gall to proposition a pregnant lady. I'm sure he's up to no good. Deputy Windam has mentioned him several times. He says he has a familiar face, but just can't place him. Let me go with you to see if we can find him."

After visiting several saloons, as they walked in the 'Ace of Clubs,' their subject was clearly playing cards with three other players. The sheriff stepped up to the man and said, "Stand up, you're under arrest. I have a complaint against you for threatening the life of a pregnant woman."

The dude stands up and says, "you're not jailing me. Step aside or you're going to get shot." As the words were spoken, Cal steps up to the man and says, "either you walk to jail, or you'll be dragged there unconscious."

"You and what army?"

Cal did a lightning draw and instead of shooting the man, he smacked the pistol's barrel on his forehead. The man's hat went flying as he collapsed to the floor. Cal looked at the patrons and said, "a silver dollar to the first two men who drag this thing to jail. As they were leaving the saloon, the bartender thanked Cal for neutralizing the dude without bloodshed or destroyed furniture.

At the sheriff's office, Cal signed an official complaint. "With this complaint, I can keep him in jail for one week without involvement of the judicial system. When he gets out, he's going to be some peed-off mad dog. So be on the lookout next Tuesday, heh."

With that in mind, Cal kept the trouble maker's hat and had Max take a good whiff of the unconscious man and his hat, for future use. He then went with the sheriff to the hotel where this Mueller look alike was staying. They could not confiscate his belongings but saw the 50X Binoculars and the Sharps rifle with a Malcolm scope. Cal understood the significance of this find, and would prepare for the man's release in one week

***

Things were hectic all week. The sheep farm was in the middle of shearing and the five men had almost 900 sheep to strip of their fleece. Clara was busy cleaning and sorting each fleece, along with the help from the two Rodriguez daughters, Maria and Isabella. Elena was operating the compressing and wrapping machine. McKnight freighting was making a full load of four bales each day. Occasionally, they would make a second load when the bales started to pile up.

The Blakely construction company was at work extending the barn and things were hopping along. One morning, Mr. McKnight arrived with two wagons. One was loaded with the new plows and harrows. On their return trip, they picked up eight wool bales to deliver at the railroad box car. The next day teams of horses, two more plows and the men to cultivate arrived at the sheep farm from the crop farm.

With extra plows, they were able to cultivate the entire 40 acres in four days, followed by a planting of winter rye to supplement the flock with high energy food before winter. With the 40 acres divided in three separate grazing pastures, Pedro was able to select the ewes and lambs for pre-winter feeding. Next spring, after passing the harrows, they would plant the grasses and forbs selected for sheep.

Cal spent all week at the crop farm. With Clara busy in the wool shop, Cal had to run the office. He and Roger often jumped in to keep the baling platform running when men took a break. Halfway thru the week, Cal had managed to do every job on the baling platform.

Roger saw a willingness for Cal to help and started training him on the horse drawn implements. Cal got the most respect when he hopped on a manure spreader that was idle because the operator had strained his back. After a long day of loading and spreading manure, Cal was glad to hear the worker would be back on the job in the AM.

During the week, Cal along with Max,

started scouting the tree line for evidence of an old lookout point. Max was able to find it quickly from the hat scent. The grass was trampled where his tripods rested just inside the tree line, and horse droppings were found 25 yards inside the tree line. This site offered an easy 500 to 600-yard shot. In preparation for Wednesday, Cal selected a hidden spot some 200 yards away, where he could spy and return fire to the assassin.

Also, in preparation, Cal went to see Ezra and purchased an old junk wooden mannequin. He dressed the mannequin in work clothing similar to what he wore regularly, including his unique hat. He then brought the dummy to the crop farm and stored it in the office's closet. He gave specific instructions for Roger and Susie to stay out of the office all day Wednesday, and to keep all doors locked.

When Wednesday arrived, Cal was at the office at pre-dawn. He placed the mannequin in the front window and locked the door. He then went to his chosen observation point and set up a rifle stand for his Win 1876 in 45-70.

He then set up his tripod to hold the 50X Binoculars. He was set up by the time the sun came up. Cal knew that Sheriff Lovering would release Mueller at the crack of dawn.

As soon as Mueller was released, he went to his hotel room and took a bath, and then had a real breakfast in the hotel restaurant. After picking up his stallion, he loaded up his gear and rifle and headed to his preselected location overlooking the crop farm office.

Cal had been patiently waiting for several hours when finally, at ten o'clock, Mueller arrived. After tethering his horse inside the trees, he started to put his gear together. He set up an upright tripod for the Sharps rifle and set up a similar tripod for his 50X Binocular glasses. As quickly as he placed his eyes to the glasses, he stepped over to the rifle. Cal could see that he had spotted the mannequin in the office window and would have an easy kill shot.

Mueller fired over the baling platform and all the workers went to ground. The bullet hit the window, shattered it, and rolled the mannequin into the far wall.

Cal had the shooter dead in his scope. Instead of shooting the assassin, he yelled, "put your hands up or your dead."

Mueller actually hopped up and turned in surprise. Squatting down, with his rifle reloaded, he was searching the tree line for a target. When Mueller appeared to be aiming at him, Cal fired and saw his target get thrown backwards. Cal slowly walked to the site and saw that Mueller was barely alive. Mueller said, "you outsmarted and killed me," as he took his last breath.

Following the old bounty hunter routine, Cal removed his pistol, gun belt, and searched his pockets and saddlebags. He found a 41 caliber derringer, two boxes of 44 ammo, one box of 41 ammo and $389 in cash. He put all the gear, rifle, binoculars and pistol back on the stallion. He would sell them later at Culligan's gun shop. He put the derringer and ammo in his own saddlebags and put the cash in his pocket. What he would do with the stallion was not yet clear.

After loading Mueller across his horse's

saddle, he rode back down to the ranch house office. As he arrived, he saw Willey Blackwell sitting next to the sheriff on a medium size wagon. Sheriff Lovering said, "shortly after releasing Mueller, I got a telegram from Denver confirming that Mueller was wanted dead or alive for kidnapping. So, I went to Willey's to get my horse, and since he was just leaving to come pick up a load of hay, I decided to hop on to come and warn you. But I see you have the package already wrapped, heh!"

"Yes, and the next time I'm in town, I'll stop by to pick up the reward voucher. This reward will go in my victim fund."

Willey volunteered to bring Mueller to the undertaker. "After the bales are loaded, we'll tie Mueller to the tailgate."

After arranging for a Blakely worker to replace the shattered window, Cal went back to his routine and ended up working the side rake all day with a large field of alfalfa ready to be picked up. As he was working the harvest, his workers were already back from the sheep farm and were cultivating the land for next year's crop.

Getting home for dinner, Clara was already in the hot tub. Cal made it clear that he was next in line and wanted a fresh tub. Installing cold and hot water in the house with a water closet was the luxury of the decade. It would make raising babies a lot easier.

They talked as they bathed, and they realized that managing and working two busy farms certainly gave them a full plate. Yet, both seemed content to continue these activities. Clara would be slowing down after the shearing and preparing for her delivery in December. Cal would be busy with the major cultivation activity until the winter freeze. By then, he would be helping Clara with housework duties to help her while nursing the baby.

Life on the eastern plains appeared to finally be a wonderful peaceful place to live, or, was this the calm before the final storm?

***

CHAPTER 9—
On the trail again

With the 40 acres of sheep pastures cultivated and planted, the continuation at the crop farm was delayed because of the oats harvesting which required mowing, bundling, threshing, winnowing and baling of the left-over straw. Afterwards, the sugar-beets were harvested and stored.

Finally, all efforts were directed at cultivation by mid-November. The full-time workers were assigned to cultivation and fertilization with phosphate and composted horse manure. Meanwhile, the seasonal workers were busy building irrigation ditches for the newly cultivated acreage.

Each day, four plows were at work and matched with disc and finish harrows. That required eight men and a dozen Belgian or Percheron draft work horses, as well as a half dozen large Gelding horses. Each day produced ten to twelve cultivated acres with a projected month's tally of +-300 new acres of cultivated land ready for spring planting.

By mid-December, the frozen earth put an end to cultivation and irrigation. The seasonal workers were laid off till spring. The eight full-time workers were reassigned. Some were helping Win repair harnesses and reshod horses, some were hauling bales along the McKnight wagons, some were maintaining implements, and some were rolling and packing the three-mile road to town and the railroad yard.

By keeping the road hard packed and frozen, freighting could continue till spring. Spring mud season would end freighting till the roads dried out.

Winter activities at the sheep farm centered on keeping the flock fed. Pedro made use of the feeding shelter with its special feeding bin that kept the wool clean of hay droppings. Each day was spent in herding the sheep to the feeding shed from the segregated paddocks. The males, barren ewes and one-year-olds were fed hay. The ewes with lambs ate alfalfa and sugar beets.

The sheep tolerated the cold because of their wool insulation. With their short legs, they did not do well in the open fields with deep snow. For that reason, the flock was kept near the feeding shed in separate paddocks. Hydration was as important as forage and for this reason, the pumps partially filled water tubs frequently to avoid freezing.

By spring, Cal knew how many bales of hay, alfalfa, straw, and the number of sugar-beets required to feed 900 sheep for 60 days when sheep could not find forage in deep snow. This year was a long time to feed the flock, but at least he knew that any increase in the flock would also need a corresponding increase in winter feed. This year's surplus would go to the local farms at a discount.

Meanwhile, at the homestead, Clara was getting heavy with child. Cal was spending more time doing household chores than going to the crop farm. Cal escorted Clara to see Doc Woodard on a regular basis. The information regarding diet, activity, and salt intake kept Clara without pregnancy related complications. The information regarding the actual delivery seemed to put Clara at ease. Cal especially appreciated the short discussion about a C-Section as a life saving measure for both mother and child. On their ride home, Cal pointed out to Clara that she was lucky— she would use a new hospital, had the benefit of a young modern surgeon, and the life long experience of an older country doctor.

Five days before Christmas, Clara went into labor. Elena escorted Clara to the Plainsville General Hospital. On arrival, Elena went with Clara and entered the Labor and Delivery Center. Cal was sent to the father's waiting room—to hurry up and wait! After a long hour without any news, Cal felt like a mushroom— kept in the dark and fed bullshit. Not getting used to the silence, Cal found himself getting wound up tight. Without any warning, the door to the labor rooms opened and startled Cal. In the doorway stood a smiling Doc Woodard who said, "Clara is four centimeters dilated, the water broke, the fetal heart is good and labor contractions are regular and strong. Mother and baby are both doing well. Any questions?"

"How long before the birth?"

"Unknown hours. I will keep you posted."

As promised, Doc Woodard came to reassure Cal several times of Clara's uncomplicated course. Four hours later, the doctor came out and said, "congratulations, you have a healthy baby and wife. Please follow me." As Cal entered a private room, he saw a sight he would never forget. Clara was smiling and holding her baby. She said, "Cal, say hello to your healthy son!"

Two days later, before taking his family home, Cal went to pay his medical bills. The receptionist was very familiar, it was Martina, now Dickson, from the victim's fund. After a short discussion of her well- being working for the doctors, Martina handed him the bill. The charges included $10 for two hospital days, $10 for Labor and Delivery, and $20 for the doctor's fee—a total of $40.

***

The winter months proved to be the most

pleasant time in the Harnell household. The baby was easily content with nursing and was changing by the week. One day Clara said, "I've found a name for our son, to honor my husband, his name will be Cal Junior with a nickname of JR." Cal shed a few tears and proudly accepted her decision.

Over the months, JR started smiling, showed facial recognition, started to crawl, started to grab objects and basically was a happy baby. When oatmeal and pureed fruits were added to his diet, Cal started feeding him.

By April, with cultivation activities restarting, Cal decided to send word to Capt. Ennis, requesting his formal resignation from the Marshal Service. The Captain sent word back accepting his resignation and thanking him for his service.

One morning, while eating breakfast with his family, Bud Hall arrived with an emergency telegram from Deputy Marshal Steve Lions, clerk for Capt. Ennis. Cal read the telegram and gave an answer to Bud, to relay back to Deputy Lions. Cal then told Clara,

"Captain Ennis and three of his Colonels were taken hostage in Brighton while attending the funeral of the retired head of the Marshal Service." Cal's services were requested in freeing the four heads of the Marshal Service. More information would be available when meeting with Deputy Lions at the Superior Hotel in Brighton.

Clara never hesitated, she placed JR in his jumper-jack and proceeded to pack Cal's gear. Cal, Max, Boss and Buster took the four- hour train to Denver and changed trains to Brighton. He arrived in Brighton at 2PM and went straight to the Superior Hotel where Deputy Lions was waiting for him in the hotel's restaurant.

"It's been two days since the Captain was expected back. Two hours ago, I received a telegram from Greeley. The abductors are holding the Captain and the three senior Marshals as hostages. They are demanding a Governor's pardon for Wilson and Ray Whitehouse or every three days, they will kill one of the hostages and leave the body in the outskirts of Greeley."

"What are the chances of a pardon?"

"I've contacted the Governor. His answer was that his office does not negotiate with criminals. With a concerned apology, he has suggested a private force to gain their release."

"Why me, why not send a half dozen Marshals to secure their release?"

"I only have six rookies in Denver and have sent telegrams to the other locations where I have capable men. It appears that all the Marshals are on the trail and not available by telegram. Now with the three-day deadline, I'm glad you're here."

"In that case, I'm off. How's the access to Greeley?"

"There is a stagecoach road directly to Greeley some 50 miles north of here."

"If I leave right away, I can be within 10— 20 miles of Greeley by nighttime. I'll keep you posted by telegram."

"I'll stay in Brighton in case some of my Marshals contact me and are available to assist you."

"Ok, but I'm not counting on them."

***

With fresh horses, Cal pushed Boss and Buster to their limits and was able to maintain a full trot and an occasional canter for the next 15 miles. He stopped in Plateville to rest the horses and get supplies at a local mercantile. Cal bought a coffee pot and frying pan. He added beans, bacon, oatmeal, hard tac, cheese, coffee and several pounds of beef jerky. Max would share the beef jerky and oatmeal. After bringing the horses to water, Cal refilled his two canteens and resumed his ride to Greeley. Max automatically jumped on Buster's dog saddle, with the supplies, and rode the remainder of the way to Greeley.

By darkness, Cal stopped and made camp some fifty yards off the trail. After removing the saddles, the horses were sent free to crop some plentiful grass. A nearby stream provided fresh water. A fire was started and Cal cooked beans and bacon for himself and a batch of oatmeal for Max. Cal retired to his bedroll after dinner, anticipating an early morning start.

Cal awakened from a deep sleep because Max was nudging him and even started to growl.

Naturally, he put his hand on his pistol that was laying next to his bedroll. Out of the stillness of the night came, "hello the camp, may I enter?"

Max bounded up and ran to the visitor. Instead of attacking him, he smelled him and then sat down in front of him. Cal stood up and noticed that the man had a rifle hung on his shoulder with a sling. "What can I do for you?"

"I've been waylaid, robbed of my money, food, pistol and horses. I've been walking for days and I'm hungry."

"How come I didn't ride past you on the stagecoach trail?"

"I heard you coming but I was afraid of again being waylaid, so I hid in the bushes till you passed. I regretted my decision after I saw your packhorse with your dog riding in a strange saddle."

"Fair enough, if my dog doesn't object to you, then I won't either. Cal holstered his Colt and said, "come in and I'll prepare you some beans, bacon and coffee."

While the coffee was boiling and the food cooking, Cal took the opportunity to get more information on the guy. "So, tell me what you're doing on the trail."

"I'm a recent widower with a ranch north of Plateville. I sold my ranch for $5,000 and placed $4,500 in the bank and kept $500 in cash. With my packhorse loaded with my personal belongings, I was on my way to Greeley to live with my only son and his family. When I was waylaid, a bear of a man beat me till I passed out. The three outlaws left me with my clothes, boots and winter jacket."

"How come you have a rifle?"

"My pappy always told me to hide one firearm when sleeping on the trail. If robbed, you still have a gun for protection. My rifle was hiding in the bushes 50 yards away, heh."

"Smart move, my name is Cal Harnell, sit down and enjoy your meal and coffee."

"Thanks, my name is Homer Westinghouse," as they shook hands.

As the man was voraciously eating, Cal asked, "is there any chance that there were more than three outlaws?"

"Yes, after I regained consciousness, as the

three thieves were gathering my stuff, I heard other horses neighing a fair distance in the woods."

"Could you recognize any of these men if you saw them again?"

"Certainly, but these are merciless and dangerous men. I rather never see their faces again."

Cal stopped talking to let the man enjoy his meal. Cal was assuming that these three outlaws were probably the abductors, along with a fourth who had been guarding the hostages. A plan was coming together in Cal's head!

By dawn, Cal and Homer enjoyed biscuits, cheese and coffee before breaking camp. Max got several pieces of jerky. Homer rode Buster bareback, without the dog saddle, and they quickly covered the estimated fifteen miles to Greeley. Arriving in town, they went to the nearest diner for a real breakfast: steak, eggs, home fries and coffee.

Waiting for their meal, Cal asked Homer what his plans were for the day. "My son's ranch is only three miles north of here. After breakfast, I'll walk over. Before I leave, how do I repay you for your help and hospitality?"

"Well I have a business proposition for you. For your help till late tonight, I will give you a saddled horse, pistol and $25 in cash. No man can arrive at his son's home without these basic survival items. I'll even include a night's stay in a hotel, so you can go to your family in the morning."

"Wow, that's an incredible deal, what do I have to do?"

"I want you to accompany me to visit every saloon in Greeley. It's my belief that we'll come up to at least one of the men who waylaid you. I need you to pick him out, and I'll take care of him."

"Is there any other reason why you need one of these outlaws."

"Yes," as he shows Homer his Marshal's badge. I'm here to rescue some Marshals held in ransom, to secure a governor's pardon, for some miscreants in the State Penitentiary."

"Lead on, I'm with you!"

"First, let's bring our horses and Max to

a livery. Then we'll start the day by getting ourselves some new clothes, and new boots for your worn-out ones. Then we'll visit a tonsorial shop for a shave, haircut, and a hot bath. Last, we'll introduce ourselves to the local sheriff before we walk the boardwalk and visit saloons."

Several hours later they walked into Sheriff Guthrie's office. Cal introduced himself as Deputy US Marshal Harnell. The sheriff was more than eager to work with a US Marshal. Cal went thru Homer's robbery and assault, as well as the abduction of the four Marshals. He even told the sheriff of their plan to locate one of the outlaws in town.

Sheriff Guthrie finally spoke, "I'm sorry, but my jurisdiction ends at the town limits. Both these crimes occurred either in Brighton or on the trail. However, if you find one of these outlaws in town, I can help you in any way you need."

"If that's the case, we'll need the use of your jail."

"That we can do, good luck and be careful."

***

By five o'clock, after a fried chicken dinner, Cal and Homer started walking the boardwalk and visiting saloons. Homer would peak over the batwing doors, if he saw no one familiar, he would walk on. At White's Gaming Bar, Homer peaked and quickly entered the saloon. He stepped to the bar with his back to gaming tables and ordered a nickel beer. Cal joined him a few minutes later and also ordered a beer. "So, what do you see?"

"Second row, first table on the right. There is a huge dude with his back to the window. He's wearing a blue shirt and red suspenders.

That's the miserable bear who beat me, while the others watched and laughed."

"Ok, let's finish our beers and leave separately. We'll meet in the back of the saloon."

Arriving at the meeting spot, Homer asked, "What's the plan to get that monster in jail?"

"We're going to wait for him to come out

to use the privy. When he does, I'll take care of him."

"Are you sure, he looks like it will take an army to bring him to his knees."

"I'll have to disable him right from the start, the rest is standard procedure to get information from him before we drag him to jail."

Over the next two hours, they saw some drunks come outside to throw up on the back lawn. Others would relieve themselves on the lawn, but most took the time to use the privy. Finally, the bear came out and went to the privy. Cal walked up to the privy's door and waited with his pistol's barrel in hand.

As the outlaw stepped out, Cal smacked him in the mouth with the pistol's butt. Several teeth went flying and the attack dropped him onto the privy's seat. Cal realized that if he stood up, he would be in trouble, so he chose to disable him from standing. Cal swung a boot to the side of the man's knee. The bear howled when his leg was bent sideways in a very unnatural position. Finally, to get control of the man, Cal pummeled him with a series of facial punches till the man lay still.

With Homer's help they dragged him by the feet some 100 yards in the woods. There, Cal slapped him into consciousness and straddled his chest. In a quick swoop, Cal opened his mouth and shoved the awl deep in a rotten molar. Both Homer and the recipient stiffened. Homer winced in pain as the outlaw screamed out and started to violently shake. Cal pulled out the awl before the man passed out.

"Ok bud, I'm only going to ask once, or you're going to get a second round in another tooth. How do I find your camp with the hostages?"

"No more! Four miles south of town, on the right side, you'll find a huge pine tree that was blown over. The roots stand eight feet high. Around the roots you'll find my trail. The camp is a mile in the woods. Now get that thing away from me."

"This tool goes away, but you're going to jail. If you lied, I'll be back for a repeat performance. When are you expected back to camp?"

"Tomorrow morning, with an answer from the Marshal Service regarding the pardon."

Cal and Homer assisted the outlaw who could not bear weight on one leg. As they arrived at the jail, Cal checked the outlaw's pockets, boots and back belt. They didn't find any knives or derringers, but they found $89 in cash and an ID for a Ben Clapper. After leaving, Cal gave Homer the $89, the outlaw's gun belt and Colt. They then went to the livery.

Cal said to the hostler. I'm a US Marshal and have arrested an outlaw that looks like a bear and is called Ben Clapper. If you have his horse, rifle, saddle, scabbard and saddlebags, I'm claiming them as mine by law."

"Fine with me, who's paying the stabling and feeding fees?"

"I will, how much and include my two horses."

"$6 total. Plus, the outlaw horse also has a shotgun with its own separate scabbard. What do I do with it?"

"Include it with the outlaw horse, and here

is $10 for your trouble. My friend's family will need a shotgun for hunting small game."

That evening after a nice dinner in the hotel restaurant, Cal said his goodbyes to Homer. "In the morning, take the cash, the guns and the saddled horse and make your way to your son. I'll be long gone when you get up, so have a nice life with your family. It's been a pleasure to make your acquaintance," as they shook hands goodbye.

***

The next morning, Cal and Max took off around 9 o'clock. This was the earliest that Clapper would have headed for camp since this was the telegraph office's opening time. Cal had no trouble finding that blown over tree. The strange thing was that Max hesitated at the site and kept looking at the other side of the road. When Cal went on the trail, Max followed.

Within minutes, Cal could smell the camp fire smoke. He tied Boss to a tree branch, took his Win 76 rifle, and quietly walked with Max toward the camp. When he heard voices, he stopped and viewed the outlaws thru his Malcolm 8X scope. To his surprise, there were five outlaws. Two were guarding the four hostages, and three were having breakfast at the camp fire.

Cal ran thru several rescuing scenarios but found that all of them would likely lead to the collateral death of one or more hostage. After careful consideration, Cal decided to rely on his shooting skills and Max as a backup. A direct confrontation would be the best way to save all the hostages.

Cal stepped forward, but Max was seen lagging behind and looking back on the backtrail. When Cal continued to walk without his rifle, Max eventually followed.

Within 25 yards of the campfire, Cal yelled, "hello the camp, I'm coming in to palaver." All the outlaws stood up and were totally surprised that a visitor had arrived without their awareness. As Max was sneaking behind the hostages, Cal spoke first.

"Your man Ben Clapper won't be coming back, he's in jail. There won't be a pardon.

Now we can do this the easy way, or the hard way. I want the hostages, and if you leave peaceably, you'll never see me again. If you decide to fight me, you'll all die."

"Them are big words for one against the five of us!"

In that moment, a shot ran out from nowhere. One of the outlaws guarding the hostages clearly stiffened with a black hole appearing on his forehead. He then crumbled to the ground and a voice was heard, "now there are four against two, them are better odds, heh. Plus, my rifle is ready to fire, and you really don't want to draw against this man or wrestle with his cur dog."

The outlaw leader was seen contemplating and then said to his man guarding the hostages, "Bull, you shoot the hostages and the three of us will take care of these two bounty hunters."

Cal saw the leader move his mouth to give his start order. Cal quickly yelled, "Max, kill." Instantaneously, Max was airborne and landed with a firm grip of Bull's neck. Max was pulling and ripped off half the outlaw's neck who landed on the ground with a spray of bright red blood.

Cal spoke again, "now it's three against me, my friend Homer will sit this out. If you draw on me, you will all die. A wise man would take his chances with a good lawyer and a fair trial. Your choice."

"If we walk away, we are dead men anyway, since the Whitehouses will eventually get their revenge." With the gunfighters beginning their draw, Cal drew his pistol and shot each outlaw in the chest before any of the outlaws cleared leather. Suddenly a shot ran out from Homer's rifle. Cal looked up and saw a man in the bushes holding a shotgun. After the rifle fire, the outlaw's shotgun lifted to the sky as he pulled both triggers during his dying throes.

After the gunfight, Cal and Homer checked and confirmed that all the outlaws were dead. As they approached the shotgun holder in the bushes, Homer said, "didn't think you had seen him next to a tree."

"I must be getting out of practice, a year ago I would not have missed that backup. As he moved to the hostages, Cal cut their bondages and removed their mouth gags. Capt. Ennis was first to speak. "I never expected you and Max, but sure glad you're here. We owe you our lives. How did you ever find us?"

"Long story for a long cup of coffee. Let's check their pockets and saddlebags for Homer's money, another long story for later." They found Homer's $500 as well as $178 which was split with Homer. They collected all the gun belts, pistols, rifles and shotgun and placed them in Homer's packhorse panniers. A total of ten boxes of 44-40 ammo was gathered which Cal would keep for his workers. Homer would also get his old riding horse and packhorse, with all the cooking utensils and his personal belongings.

While they were loading all the dead bodies on their horses, Cal asked Homer, "how in blazes did you know where the camp was and how did you follow me without my knowing it?"

"It was a full moon last night and at 2 AM I rode down the road looking for that down pine. When I found it, I moved 50 yards across the road and waited for you. When you arrived at the pine tree, Max almost gave me away because of my scent. I walked and followed you along the trail, and Max again sensed my presence as you stepped off your horse. He again almost gave me away but for some strange reason he didn't for the second time. The rest is history."

The caravan arrived in Greeley. Six dead outlaws splayed over their saddles, Homer's two extra horses, the four hostages on horseback and lead by Cal and Homer. Sheriff Guthrie had the name of the outlaws thanks to the cooperation of Ben Clapper. He would wire Western Union with their ID and see if there were any rewards on their heads.

Capt. Ennis and the three Colonels were planning to take the stagecoach back to Brighton and then switch to the train to Denver. Since the stagecoach did not leave for two hours, Cal invited them to the diner for lunch. Waiting for their order, Capt. Ennis said, "I didn't expect you since you're officially retired. How come you got involved?"

"It's a long story as I said, but thanks to your

determined and wise clerk, Deputy Lions, I could not refuse his request for assistance. Let's call it payback. You accepted me as a bounty hunter and later as a special deputy. This is my thanks for your trust in me. Now let's eat."

After the stagecoach departed, Cal and Homer proceeded to dispose of the outlaw horses. Two liveries purchase all ten horses for a total of $500. A local gun shop was eager to purchase the six pistols, five rifles and one shotgun. Cal was offered $25 for each Colt pistol, #35 for each Win 73 rifle and $30 for the shotgun. Cal said he would think about it and decide before leaving town.

The last place to visit was the sheriff's office. Sheriff Guthrie asked Cal for $40 to pay the undertaker, which Cal paid. He then hands Cal seven Western Union Vouchers, including the voucher for Ben Clapper. Six were for $500 and one was for the leader worth $1,500. Cal hands Sheriff Guthrie $100 for the use of the jail until the prisoner was transferred to Brighton for trial.

As they left the sheriff, Cal hands Homer

two of the $500 vouchers. "This is your money for shooting those two outlaws, not to say you saved my life. I'll be leaving today, so let's say goodbye for the second time. If you ever get sick of retirement, come and see me in Plainsville. I'm sure I can find you a position as a crop farmer, a sheep farmer or a lawman."

As they were saddling their horses and were departing in different directions, Cal had the strange feeling that he would see this man again.

***

CHAPTER 10— A New Career

Before leaving Greeley, Cal changed his mind and decided to keep the five pistols, six rifles and one shotgun. He packed them and added them to Buster's panniers. After serious consideration, he was beginning to develop an idea he needed to discuss with Clara.

Cal made his way to the railroad depot in Denver and boarded the passenger train to Plainsville with Boss, Buster and Max in the stock car. Cal sat in the second row of double seats. In front of him was a couple with an older man. Also, across the isle was another couple with an older man. Both women appeared young and Cal doubted they were of the legal age of eighteen. As the train was traveling, Cal could hear the conversation of the couple in front of him.

It became clear that this young lady was to be a mail order bride. She asked several questions about the man she was to marry. Some of the answers given did not make sense. When the lady asked what her husband to be did for a living, the man said that he owned a gold mine in Sterling. Cal doubted that there were gold mines in the plains surrounding Sterling. Other parts of the conversation sounded fabricated to placate the young lady. Cal's hackles were finally up when the lady got up to go to the privy and the older man escorted her to the privy. A bit later, the other young lady went to the privy. Her escort stayed in his seat till the man in front of Cal signaled him to follow his apparent charge.

As they arrived in Sterling, the Conductor announced that there would be a three-hour delay because a faulty steam valve needed to be replaced. The two couples got up and Cal decided to follow them. As they walked the boardwalk, they passed several locations where they could have met their intended mates. They passed the courthouse, municipal building and several churches. That is when Cal knew that these men were up to no good.

As anticipated, they stopped in front of Madame Lizette's House of Pleasure. The two ladies became combative but were both violently knocked out before they were carried through a side entrance door. Cal made his way to the front entrance and was greeted by Madame Lizette.

"What is your pleasure today?"

"I just saw two ladies carried thru your side entrance. I don't like what I saw and insist on speaking to them."

Madame Lizette said, "certainly, wait here and I will get them." She stepped out and returned with two 300-pound bouncers. The lead gorilla leaned against a table and placed both hands on the table. He then told Cal that if he didn't leave, that he would be thrown out. Cal smiled and out of nowhere, the awl went smacking on the bouncer's hand. It perforated the hand and impaled itself deep in the table top. The look of shock on his face with a wide-open mouth was then followed by a scream of horror. The second bouncer stepped up to Cal ready to crush his face as Cal drew his pistol and planted the barrel onto the bouncer's forehead. Cal then applied handcuffs and pulled out his Marshal's badge.

"Ma'am, you have thirty seconds to tell me where the ladies are or you're going to jail."

"They are with the two men who brought them here. Second floor, first room on the left."

Cal went up the stairs, two steps at a time and quietly opened the designated door to view inside the room. He saw both ladies spread eagle, tied hands and feet to bedposts, gagged and complexly naked. Both men were naked, one was already crawling over one of the girls getting ready to rape her, the other was preparing himself to do the same. Cal kicked the door in, the man standing turned around holding his manhood, Cal drew his pistol and shot him in the foot. He collapsed to the floor screaming and holding his bleeding foot. At the same time, the other man turned around as Cal grabbed both feet and yanked him off the lady. In the process the man was pulled over the foot of the steel bed and his testicles got crushed in the process. He then laid on the floor holding his privates as Cal gave him a round punch to the nose and knocked him out. Handcuffs were applied to both men.

Cal stepped up to the gals, covered them with a sheet, removed their gags and cut their restraints. "You are now both free, get dressed while I take care of these two kidnappers." Cal dragged both naked men into the hall and closed the bedroom door to give the gals some privacy.

As he was contemplating what to do with all four men, the local sheriff and two deputies showed up to investigate the gun shot. Cal introduced himself as a Deputy US Marshall. The sheriff immediately smiled and said, "I know who you are, but I heard you retired."

"That is correct, but I could not let a kidnapping go." Cal told the entire story to the sheriff. The sheriff said, "the two downstairs will automatically get ten days in jail for threatening a lawman. Madame Lizette will be fined for improperly acquiring ladies of the night, and these two kidnappers will go to trial with a statement from you and the two victims. If there is no plea deal, you and the victims will need to return for the trial."

"Agree, this one will need care for the hole in his foot, and the one downstairs will also need care for the hole in his hand, after I take my awl back."

"Ok boys get these turds dressed and bring all four to jail. Get the doc to attend to the injured ones."

"After I talk to the victims, I will meet you at your office to write our statements and get my handcuffs back"

"Meanwhile, I'll check with Western Union, these kidnappers may have a price on their heads."

***

"Well ladies, welcome to freedom and a new life. My name is Cal Harnell."

"I'm Gail Stevens." "And I'm Samantha Pierce."

"How old are you gals?"

With some pause, Gail admits, "we're both seventeen and a half."

"I figured as much. Are you hungry?"

"Yes, we are famished, we only had crackers and oatmeal yesterday."

"Well, we have plenty of time before the train departs, so let's find a diner and get a late lunch."

They all ordered the special: meatloaf, mashed potatoes, turnip, coffee and a dessert of bread pudding. Waiting for their meal, Cal asked them for their life's story. The gals alternated, since their story was the same.

Gail started, "we were both orphaned at age thirteen when our parents and siblings died of cholera. The only orphanage to take teenagers was a private facility called 'the Metcalfe Home. We were required to work every morning. The jobs were not the best. The older boys emptied privies or picked up horse manure on the streets. The girls emptied chamber pots in the hotels or did their laundry."

Samantha took over, "the owners of the home were paid for our work, we in turn were given some schooling every afternoon. Gail and I were lucky, since age 15 we worked in a general mercantile. We stocked the shelves, cleaned the floor, unloaded supplies and even assisted customers. I took care of dry goods and clothing and Gail took care of hardware. We were both able to work the cash and books on credit."

"Why do you want to know."

"It's a long story, but I take care of victims. You are both victims and I will find you a job and a place to live. Not in Sterling but in my home town of Plainsville. Now let's eat and get back to the sheriff's office for our statements and then the train."

With statements finished, Cal was handed two $500 vouchers. It appeared that these two miserable individuals were also wanted for human trafficking of under age women. The sheriff in turn would notify the Denver police that the Metcalfe Home was selling girls into a scam mail order bride scheme.

"Did you know that you had been bought into slavery?"

"No, all we knew was that the Metcalfe Home had to discharge us at age 18. Guess they saw a chance to make some money beyond our wages. We thought they were so kind to find us a wealthy husband and a home. We won't be so naïve in the future."

Arriving in Plainsville, the girls appeared anxious until Cal started directing their activities. "First, we are going to buy you a pistol for self- defense. They stopped at Culligan's gun shop and Cal bought two Webley Bulldog. Ken, the owner, was paid for the pistols, with two shoulder holsters, and a two-hour course on how to shoot them safely. During the transaction, Cal noted that Ken and Samantha seemed to eye each other when they thought no one was watching.

Their next stop, Ezra's Mercantile. "Now girls, you need dresses, britches, riding pants, undergarments, personal hygiene items, beauty accessories, boots, shoes and a western hat. If I missed anything, get them."

"While the girls were shopping, Cal visited with Ezra. "How is business?"

"Very busy, the town is growing. Even with my son opening the hardware section, I'll need some help. However, I'm a bit short of cash to pay some help. I have too many accounts on credit, because of hard times. That makes ordering supplies difficult."

"Well, I can help you with that. Let me tell you about my victim account...............So, give me the total due on all accounts over $50."

"That comes to $1721."

"Here is a voucher for $3,000. Pay them off and help anyone who is not ordering what they need because of asking for credit. When you need more, let me know. Please keep my name as an anonymous benefactor."

"Oh, my goodness, this is unbelievable. I will now look for some help. Thank you."

"As far as help, see that young lady picking out some clothes. She has experience working in a mercantile. As a favor to me, would you consider hiring her?"

"Be glad to, what is her name?"

"Samantha Pierce. To help your finances, pay her salary out of the $3,000 for the next six months."

As the girls brought their clothes to the cash register, Cal sent them back saying, "I want you to have a complete wardrobe, not just a few items."

As they left the mercantile, Samantha had a job and both gals had a proper array of garments and footwear. Gail then asked, "how can we ever pay you back?"

"It's part of your victim package. There is no payback necessary. Now let's go find Gail a job."

After entering "Forks and Wrenches," Cal had a private talk with Lyle and he made him an offer he could not refuse. Gail was hired on the spot. Upon leaving, Cal said, "now let's find you a place to live with meals included."

They went to Myrtle's Rooming House and they accepted a large room with two beds and all meals included for $40 a month. Cal paid for six months in advance and the girls moved in with their clothes. When Cal was prepared to leave, both girls were full of tears. Cal said, "I'll be checking on you whenever I'm in town, but if you need anything go see Sheriff Lovering and he'll help you or notify me. Finally, here is each $50 in cash for your other needs till you get your first paycheck."

On his way home, Cal stopped to see Sheriff Lovering and informed him about Gail and

Samantha. The sheriff took the opportunity to breach a subject with Cal. "A few days ago, Dan Whitehouse came to see me. Since the recent abduction failed to get them a pardon, he fears that his father and brother would try another ploy to get them a pardon. I suspect they will try something at your home. Please stay vigilant and let me know if something happens."

In view of this information, Cal sent a telegram to Captain Ennis regarding an idea becoming again more apropos. He then proceeded home to his wife and son.

Arriving home, Clara was all tears. "I'm so glad you're back and I have some good news. Doc Woodard said it was safe to resume relations but that I would be highly fertile."

"I'm glad to hear that, but would a pregnancy this soon be a hazard to your health?"

"No, actually he suggested that the time to build our family was when I was young and healthy. Besides, I have no fear with child birth with Doc Woodard providing my care."

Cal went in the nursery, picked up JR and carried him all over the house. JR recognized his dad and smiled when he saw him. Eventually, they all sat at the kitchen table and Clara wanted to know how the emergency assignment went. Cal started talking. "It was an enlightening event." As Clara's eyebrows went up.

"When I caught up with the kidnappers, I identified five outlaws holding the hostages. With Max taking care of one, I knew I could outdraw four of them. However, when the time came to shoot, I forgot there was another outlaw sitting outside of camp with a shotgun. I don't know if I was overconfident, reckless or preoccupied, but a year ago I would not have missed that sixth gun in the bushes."

"Oh no, what saved you?"

"A man I had helped on the trail, a long story, decided to follow me and assist me if necessary. He fortunately shot one of the outlaws as well as that sixth man. He saved my life, Clara!"

"What does that mean for the future?"

"Before I get to that, let me tell you about another caper on the train ride to home." After a long story, Clara asked its significance.

"I just can't get away from letting criminals

abuse good people. It's become what I am. I'm very involved with our two farms and happily committed to you and JR. Yet I need to continue being a responsible lawman and I believe I have found an enterprise where I can incorporate farms, family life and a private detective/lawman agency."

"What an idea, tell me more."

"Before coming home, I sent a telegram to Capt. Ennis. I asked him if I should reinstate my Deputy Marshal status. I also asked him to send me a list of eligible men who would be willing to move to Plainsville and sign up in my training class. Once they graduate, they would become independent police officers in my agency. Their pay would be a major share of the financial bounties on the head of each criminal, dead or alive. If our agency provided a paper service for the government or the Marshal Service, our men would be paid a fixed daily amount. There would be many details to be worked out."

"How would such an agency provide more safety for you or your men?"

"Because no man would leave my office

without a backup. Even delivering an overdue notice can be dangerous since people think that shooting the messenger will make their bills go away. If a gunfight is possible, we'll increase the number of men according to the need. Depending on the situation, I will join my men on more dangerous assignments."

"You have my complete support. What are you going to call the agency?"

"The Harnell Security Agency.

"Ok, dinner time, your son is hungry. Let's hope you get a positive response from Capt. Ennis."

After nursing the baby, Clara served a vegetable beef stew with biscuits and coffee. Dessert consisted of bearpaw pastries, Cal's favorite. As they were cleaning the dishes, a telegraph messenger showed up with a long telegram from Capt. Ennis.

From: Capt. Ennis
Denver Marshall Service
To: Cal Harnell
Plainsville, CO.

A private enterprise excludes you from Marshal Service STOP

The Rainbow Agency was sold but there are problems STOP

Foreman Clarence Simpson and three others quit STOP

Offered them a Deputy Marshal position. But refused STOP

These good men want to work on commission, not salary STOP

Four men are taking the train tomorrow to speak with you STOP

Given circumstances, would use your agency—good luck STOP

***

The next morning, after a night of marital bliss, Clara said, "I'm certain that I am pregnant!"

"Well no one can deny that there was plenty of rolling and shaking. I doubt the ovaries could take the pounding." As Clara came into his arms laughing and kissing him.

"What are your plans for the day."

"I think I'm going to visit Pedro and Roger until those men arrive from Boulder." After a replenishing breakfast, Cal went to see Pedro.

"How are things going?"

"We had a good wool harvest and the fleeces are all gone to the Denver market and mills. Things were quiet, we had wiped out the predators, then some animals stopped eating and develop diarrhea. Benjamin had the sheep droppings analyzed by Doc Woodard and they found something called a parasite."

"We are now treating the affected ones with a liquid obtained at the hardware store. I can tell you that in the old days, this type of problem would have killed 25% of adults and 50% of lambs. It's been three days on the medicine and the diarrhea is slowing down. The affected ones are still separated in a different pasture which has stopped the spread of the problem. We are fortunate that Benjamin is working for us. Otherwise, we're feeding the sheep and waiting for spring."

Moving to the crop farm, Roger was busy in the office looking at some new magazines on farm implements. "Well hello Roger, you look like a man trying to solve a problem."

"As I'm planning ahead, this is the situation. With four plows we'll have 450 acres ready for spring planting. By harvest time we'll have an extra 150 acres cultivated for a total of 600 harvestable acres, with 40 acres of mature pine and fir trees. Can you imagine harvesting 600 acres between +-July 1 to +-October 30—plus two weeks for threshing oats and baling straw."

"Yes, that's what our goal has always been. What do you need to make this happen?"

"Well here is a list, just as a starter:

1. Double the number of year-round workers.

2. Triple the number of seasonal workers.

3. Double the implements, that's four mowers, four balers and two of every implement in-between.

4. Buy some gasoline motors to operate the balers instead of horses turning a cam. Each unit will be at least 30% more efficient and the spare four horses will have plenty of work. These four freed

up horses will allow us not to purchase more horses for now.

5. Double the number of feed-store retailers and or crop distributors in Denver or beyond.

6. Have Silas double his freighting company.

7. Ask the railroad to be more diligent in exchanging their loaded box cars for empty ones. They tend to hold us up.

8. We'll need to expand the bunkhouse or build a second one."

"Done, I'll take care of finding more retailers/distributors, get Silas to double the number of freighting wagons, and arrange a contract with the railroad manager for better service. You take care of the rest."

Roger hesitates and says, "well as usual, that's fair enough, heh." As they both break down in laughter.

"All kidding aside, that's a lot of work. I believe you need help. It's time for you to upgrade your best man and make him your foreman. You'll be the general manager and I'll be the 'silent owner,' heh."

"The man I want is thinking of leaving because he's getting married. I've been trying to convince him to live in town and ride the three miles to work, but that idea is not going well."

"You never loose a good man. Build him a house next to yours so you can at least use the same windmill/well. That's what we did with Pedro and we never regretted it. Seal the deal with a pay raise if you have to. Remember, a foreman on the premises is worth three men living in town."

"Well Cal, we have a deal. We are no longer just a crop grower, we are now going to be a full-fledged commercial crop grower."

"One last item. Are any of the workers complaining of their pay?"

"I have not heard a single complaint. Whenever there are some, usually they complain to the stable man, but Win says that everyone is in a good mood. However, you do realize that 90% of our workers now go to church on Sunday because you guaranteed their full-days' pay. Yet they are all back by lunch time at noon. Now, Ezra stays open till noon on Sunday because so many workers get their personal supplies on Sunday morning. Before and after church, of course, heh."

"As long as they have the work ethics to be back by noon, I'm ok with that."

"There is no doubt, Cal, this is a great place to work. The proof, all the workers volunteer and do their share in helping the men who haul manure. I've noticed a pleasant comradery amongst the workers."

"Ok, let's move on to the final expansion."

***

The next morning, Cal was at the railroad depot to meet Clarence Simpson and his associates. As Clarence stepped onto the platform, he spotted Cal and walked to greet him. As they shook hands, Clarence said, "nice to see you again. Strange how these things go around and come back around!"

"I'm glad you're here. Introduce me to your friends."

"As you can see, I have one experienced man by the name of Floyd Young who worked for you last year, and two one-year old rookies by the name of Larry Bullock and Jim Betts." After shaking hands, Cal brought the men to Bessie's Diner for breakfast.

Once the orders were in, Cal asked Clarence to give his story of why they had quit the Rainbow Agency, and what they were looking for as far as work.

"Eric Alderson sold the Rainbow Agency to a ruthless, heartless, money hungry bully. He only cares about money and has no interest in the safety or wellbeing of his men. He has already cut our daily pay by 50% to $2.50 and our bounty rewards to 25% from 40%. He doesn't care if an assignment is dangerous, he won't add extra men. I hate to admit that we lost several good men last month and he does not provide any financial support for the surviving dependents."

"The real difficulty is his organization. Eric Alderson had hired his men according to their abilities. That way he had four divisions:

process servers, trackers, protection and gunfighters. Every man was comfortable in his own division. Now, this man has abandoned all these divisions and is expecting each man to perform all the jobs—without any additional training."

"Those are the reasons we quit and are looking for work."

As the hardy breakfast of steak and eggs arrived, they ate with few words. Afterwards, with plenty of coffee to go around, Cal took over. "I plan to build a private agency that is a mixed breed of bounty hunter—lawman—and security. I want two teams of two men each. Each team leader will have a backup man. I will train each man for all the jobs that this agency will handle: process servers, gunfighters, security guards and trackers."

"The training will last one month and will include nine different categories:

- Shooting proficiency with short- and long-range shot gunning, short range pistol shooting and 100-300-yard rifle shooting. I will not teach you the art of fast draw. You'll have a sawed-off shotgun for a gunfight.

- We'll cover the proper way to serve processes and write reports.
- The tricks to tracking.
- How to detect and handle an ambush on the trail.
- How to set up a safe camp on the trail.
- How to win a gunfight.
- How to set up a protection ring.
- How to perform a safe arrest on the trail or in a building.
- How to bring outlaws, on the trail, safely to jail.

"Now let's get down to specifics with a Question/Answer approach."

Q. "What is our pay?"

A. "$5 a day when on assignment. 40% of all reward money split amongst the team members."

Q. "What do we do when there's no work?"

A. "No work, no pay. However, if you go to outlying towns and look at their wanted posters and talk to local lawmen, I will pay half your day rate plus all your expenses."

Q. "So why make our base in Plainsville? Why not Denver?"

A. "Because I live here, I have two businesses here, and we have the railroad and telegraph in town. We can be anywhere in the State in one day by train."

Q. "What is our cost for the training?"

A. "You got it wrong. I'll pay you $100 for the month. I will also provide room and board in my crop farm bunkhouse. That's where we'll hold class, on my range and in my office."

Q. "Do we get insurance if we get hurt or shot?"

A. "Half pay till you get back to work."

Q. "What are our expenses?"

A. "None when you're working. That's the reason you get 40% of the reward money. 20% goes to travel expenses (train fares, hotels and meals etc.) and your disability insurance. I get 40% but half goes in my victim fund and half in my personal account."

Q. "What happens if we get killed on the job and have dependents?"

A. "Let me explain the victim fund................. Your family will qualify for my victim fund and will be supported for life.

Q. "Where do we live?"

A. "Here's a deal. Live in my bunkhouse with full meals. In return, if there is no work, work on my crop farm 3-5 days a month to pay for your room and board. If there is agency work, it cancels your work days on the farm."

Q. "What about the ones with families, where do we live?"

A. "Rent a house in town. Don't buy. I'll pay you an automatic $40 to compensate your expenses. Assuming things work out, stay with me for one year and I'll build you a house free of charge on my crop farm."

Q. "How do we choose the teams?"

A. "I will. During the training month, I'll match your individual abilities to complement each other. I guarantee that each team will have an experienced man with a rookie."

Q. "Some private agencies have a company uniform. Does that include us?"

A. "Yes and no. I'll provide black pants, a dark blue hickory shirt, a black hat, a dark vest and a badge of my design. As a team with the Harnell Security badge and matching attire, it provides stealth on the trail and some respect when dealing with the public. You'll always carry a second set of clothes for routine undercover work."

Q. Clarence tells me that I need to trade my stallion for a gelding. Why is that so important?"

A. "Let's say you're sneaking up onto an outlaw camp and one of the outlaws has a mare. Your stallion or their mare will start nickering and ruin your stealth mode. Not too smart, heh. I agree with Clarence."

As the meeting came to an end, it was clear that all four men were pleased with the offer. They agreed to return in a week, with their gear, horses and guns to spend the month in Cal's bunkhouse. They all shook hands and took the train back to Boulder.

Before going home, Cal went to see Ken Culligan at his gun shop. As he entered, he saw Samantha working the receiving counter. "What are you doing working here, I thought you worked for Ezra?"

"Ken needed a front person one day a week, so he could catch up on the back log of gun repairs. So now I work six and a half days a week since Ezra is open Sunday till noon. I'm very happy and I really like Ken."

"Great, now I'd like to place a special order which I will need in one week. Four coach 12-gauge shotguns, four 12-gauge sawed-off shotguns, four backpack holsters for the sawed-off shotguns, four Win 1876 rifles, four Webley Bulldog, scabbards for the rifles and coach shotguns and shoulder holsters for the Bulldogs. A case of 44-40 ammo, half a case of 45-70 ammo and twenty 25 round boxes of 12-gauge shells."

"Ken got a huge order three days ago. Let me see what we have."

Samantha returned in a few minutes. "We have everything in stock except the sawed-off shotgun backpack holsters. Ken will modify the four shotguns to your specs and the next-door leather shop will have the backpack holsters in three days. Come back in five days and your order will be ready. Your total comes to: coach shotguns $120, sawed-off shotguns $160, backpacks $40, Win 1876 $200, eight scabbards $160, case of 44-40 $20, half case of 45-70 $25, twenty boxes of mixed OO and #3 Buck $20. Ken added four slides holding

45-70 and shotgun shells—free. If my math is correct it comes to $865." Cal paid with a bank voucher and added $20 for Silas to deliver his order when ready.

A week later the four men arrived with all their gear. Cal gave them a full day to get use to the hustle and bustle of the crop farm. The next morning Cal started his program after breakfast.

"As a general routine, every day we'll start with class time till 11 o'clock when we'll spend an hour on the range. After lunch, we may again start with class time and go back to the range at 4 o'clock till dinner. Or, we may have an afternoon of just shooting practice. Repeated short practices is one of the best ways to train your muscles into a memory and functional pattern."

Today we start with shooting skills. Other than a short discussion, we'll spend the next two full days doing extensive training, and as mentioned, for the rest of the month we'll practice twice a day."

SHOOTING SKILLS

PISTOLS. "I'm not teaching the art of fast draw. This is not a skill you'll need to do your job. Fast draw is a life long technique with some natural abilities. Instead I will emphasize acquired skills."

"For safety reasons, only load five rounds with an empty chamber under the hammer, and always keep the hammer loop in place. When going to a possible shootout, load the sixth chamber and release the hammer loop."

"I expect you to be able to hit a man size target, single handed, at ten short paces by the point and shoot method. If you have to use your pistol at 25 yards, take careful aim and support the pistol with your left hand."

"The Webley Bulldog is for undercover work. At such times, you dress in normal Cowboy attire, with a vest to hide the pistol in the shoulder holster. This will allow you to be armed without the obvious appearance of carrying a firearm."

SHOTGUNS. "The sawed-off shotgun is for short distances of +-ten short paces. You'll learn to draw it out of your backpack holster, cock the hammers and present it with both hands for pointing and shooting. Load it with #3 buckshot for the extra pellets over OO Buck. Whether you shoot one or both barrels will be discussed during training."

"The coach shotgun, loaded with OO Buckshot, is reliable up to +-40 yards. Most of these current shotguns have different barrels. One is usually full choke and the other is modified. Test the diameter of the muzzle with a coin to determine which is which. The front trigger usually fires the right barrel, and the rear fires the left barrel. This shotgun will do the same as the sawed- off one but is best used for longer distances. As an example, if you're 'riding shotgun' on a stagecoach, use the coach shotgun."

1873 RIFLE. "This is a 100-yard gun. Learn to shoot it 'off hand' since a rest is not always available. I expect you to hit a 5-gallon pail at 100 yards. Always keep the magazine fully loaded but without a round in the chamber—only rack the lever when you need to."

1876 RIFLE. "This is a long-range rifle, up to 400 yards with the use of a 8X Malcolm telescope. Through the scope, you'll learn to differentiate the man size target at different distances. This type of shooting is best done on a rifle rest. Since most of you have not done much long-range shooting, we'll practice this one till you're proficient. I can attest to the fact, that picking off a sniper at 300 yards, has saved my bacon several times. You'll learn to change the scope settings to accommodate the different yardages."

"On a final note, always keep spare ammo on your body. Here is a slide that fits on your gun belt. It holds 45-70 ammo and shotgun shells. Your spare 44-40 ammo should be on your gun belt. So, lets start our training with the pistols. After lunch we'll move to the shotguns and rifles. Tomorrow, we'll practice all day."

<u>Shooting skills.</u> In the first hour, Cal realized that all four men needed help. They all admitted that with their 'protection division,' they had relied on the rifle. They all had a slow draw, a fumbled hammer pull, and 75% misses. Cal spent a considerable amount of time showing them the proper method and sequence to get their handgun onto a stable point and shoot position. In one hour, all four men had mastered the proper technique and future practices would increase their proficiency.

The Bulldog pistol seemed easier to handle. They liked the fact that a double action pistol did not need the hammer pulled back to fire— just pull the trigger. They were accurate with this pistol from the start. Of course, they were shooting at a man size target only six feet away. After lunch, Cal tackled the shotguns. After showing them how to pull the sawed-off shotgun out of the backpack, they quickly mastered this firearm. They all appreciated that this was a defensive as well as an attack weapon. Cal thought how that was good news, since this would become their "go to gun." He pointed out that brandishing this lethal weapon to an outlaw not only demanded respect but would often prevent a shootout.

The coach shotgun was a surprise to everyone. At 40 yards, a man size target would have three pellet hits out of a possible nine of OO Buckshot. Cal had them practice shooting the 40-yard target on a run—to simulate shooting from a horse, wagon or stagecoach. It took quite a while for them to start getting hits. At the end of the shotgun training, these non-shotgun users were changing their minds about the value of this weapon—as Cal expected.

The 1873 rifle needed no training. Every man could easily hit a five-gallon pail at 100 yards. Their past use of this rifle during their work on the protection division gave them all the experience they needed. They would not waste much ammo on this firearm.

The 1876 rifle was another matter. The report and recoil of a 45-70 round got their undivided attention, to say the least. It was also a new experience to look thru an 8X scope and see the difference in a man size target at 100, 200, 300, and 400 yards. Cal had to show them the proper breathing and trigger control to do this kind of shooting.

With their scope set at 200 yards, Cal had calculated the drop of a 350-grain bullet at 300 and 400 yards. This drop was compensated by the elevation dial. In time, each man could quickly change from one yardage to another. Cal realized that this type of shooting would require a lot of practice and many rounds downrange.

The next day, Cal changed his mind and dedicated the next two full days for shooting practice. They needed to be good with the guns that would save their lives. The men were shooting 2000 rounds a day. When the cook announced he was going to town for supplies, Cal asked him to bring back 4000 rounds of the mixed cartridges and shells.

<u>Serving processes.</u> Finally, the fourth day arrived and was dedicated to serving processes. "As a security agency, for a fee, we serve papers

generated by the court, the tax collector, the land office, merchants, lawyers and occasionally even the sheriff."

"The standard method of serving anyone is to address them as, 'We were ordered and sent here by the court to deliver these papers to you, you've been served.' If the recipient takes the papers and says, 'what is this?' it's because the person can't read and then you have to explain what the papers are before you politely take your departure."

"Why do we need two agents to serve processes?"

"Because without a show of force or authority, the messenger risks getting a beating—as a message to the sender. When your backup is holding a shotgun, you'll be able to depart intact, heh." Cal then showed them examples of documents they would be serving: a court summons, a divorce announcement, over due bills to merchants, over due taxes, bank or tax foreclosures, law suits and a few others."

"Why would we serve processes for the sheriff?'

"A court ordered arrest warrant is often a problem since the sheriff may not have the manpower to do this safely."

"Are we going to have to do many of these processes?"

"Probably not since we still live in a small town. Yet it's income between major assignments."

"What do you think will be our major assignments?"

"Gangs. Very dangerous outlaws with big prices on their heads. That's why I'm putting you thru all this training!"

Tracking. "We all know that American Indians are the best trackers. Yet most of the time, you'll have to rely on yourselves. Even if you aren't a natural talent, you can all track using these acquired tips."

1. "Deep front end shoe marks usually means a horse on the run."
2. "When all shoe marks are deep, expect two riders on the horse."

3. "Light tracks usually means a trailing horse or a packhorse."

4. "Look for a defective shoe, it keeps you on the proper track."

5. "Going cross-country, look for flattened or disturbed grasses when hoof marks are not easily visible."

6. "When in wooded areas, look for broken branches."

7. "Check the temperature and dryness of manure, to give you an idea of how close you're getting."

8. "The dryness of the shoe marks will tell you if you're hours or days behind."

9. "Check the layout of the horses. Four tracks of four outlaws going to three tracks means an ambush may be ahead."

10. "A light shoe mark means a limping horse."

11. "The size of the shoe reflects the horse size but also the man's size."

12. "Outlaws will tend to ride thru a stream. Each of you take a side and travel at a trot till you find their exit. A hint, often

when they enter on one side, they'll exit on the same side."

13. "Rocky land provides the greatest tracking challenge. Slow your horse down to a walk or even walk next to your horse. Look for certain signs: disturbed stones, scratches on stone, an occasional shoe mark on a patch of earth or a disturbed plant or grassy patch."

14. "Maintain a riding speed that matches your ability to keep on track. If you're riding too fast, you'll lose the track and waste precious time."

"As you can see, tracking is a perpetually learning experience. Use your partner's ideas and eyes. In addition, every tracking event provides its own unique situation. I'm certain that you have your own little tricks, so let's hear them so we can all benefit."

After a long discussion, lunch came up. After lunch, back to shooting practice for the remainder of the day.

<u>Ambush.</u> "An ambush on the trail is the most dangerous part of following outlaws. Outlaws have no morals. Shooting you in the back is their way. They are cowards who just want to kill you, so they can go on their way without risking their necks."

"Surviving an ambush requires you to spot a likely location or 'feel it.' To detect a location, look for an area with large trees, gullies and boulders. Avoid riding thru a sharp curve without checking it out. To 'feel it,' you have to start thinking like an outlaw. If your partner is suspecting an ambush, believe him and deal with it."

"And how do we manage an expected ambush?"

"OK, let's say you arrive at a suspicious location. Stop and perform your routine: *The rear man stays in place and holds his coach shotgun at port arms, loaded with OO Buck and ready to shoot. The lead man moves ahead at a medium trot while holding his shotgun over his saddle. As soon as the lead man passes the hidden outlaw, the outlaw will stand up and aim his rifle at the lead man's back. That instant is when a quick response is needed from the man in the rear. He must quickly shoot at the outlaw with one barrel followed by a second shot. Out of 18 pellets, he'll get several hits. It's then up to the lead man to turn his horse around quickly and finish the outlaw."*

This is a real life-saving routine. We will practice this on the range with horses till each team can master each position. We'll even add variables such as distances and exposure of the outlaw to each man."

"Prevention is an alternative, so what can we do to avoid an ambush?"

"The only reason outlaws set up an ambush is because they know you're on their backtrail. So, don't start a campfire, don't ride too fast to raise a dust cloud, don't ride with a posse, if you can see them, they can see you, if you use binoculars, they should be shielded with leather rims to prevent light reflection, don't talk too loud since your voices carry in the plains, don't ride a white horse, and always wear your uniform since it's perfect camouflage."

"If the outlaws don't know you are trailing them, you will eventually be able to sneak up on them in their camp."

<u>The Safe Camp.</u> "If you can sneak up on outlaws, they can do the same to you while in your camp. More good men are lost because of the assumption that you'll awaken if you have visitors. WRONG."

"Whenever on the trail, you need to follow a routine to minimize the chances of a surprise attack from the outlaws you're chasing or other miscreants who want to rob and kill you. This has been my routine for the past two years, and it's saved my life several times."

1. "Set your camp 50 yards off the road. Try to get a location with trees or boulders at your back and fresh water/ grass for your horses."

2. "Keep your horses close to camp, they can warn you of visitors, of the two and four-legged kind."

3. "Start a small fire by digging a firepit. Use dry twigs to minimize smoke. Once your dinner and coffee are done, douse the fire out."

4. "Your camp center is where your saddles are located. So, make a fake bedroll with your tarp full of grass or bushes. Leave the fake bedrolls near the saddles and put your real bedroll at least twenty yards away—preferably in the trees, behind boulders or heavy brush."

5. "Always carry this reel of cord and these cowbells. Surround your camp with the cord strung out some six inches off the ground. Hook the cowbells to the right and left of the likely entrance points. Anyone walking in your camp will have a real surprise when they trip on the cord."

6. "Last, your best firearm in any camp is your sawed-off shotgun. Keep it next to your bedroll."

7. "The only exception to the campfire routine is winter months. You need a fire, or you'll get sick."

<u>Protection ring.</u> "This one we'll skip. The four of you have been in this division and two of you worked for me when Clara needed protection. I saw how you set yourselves up and I liked what I saw. So, let's move on to the gunfight."

<u>The Gunfight.</u> "There will come a time when you'll be 'called out' by some desperate outlaws determined to fight it to the end in a face to face gunfight. If you stick to this defense, you'll put down the threat every time. Remember, a gunfight is not a match that has to be a noble event. You are defending yourself and can use whatever method will achieve that goal."

"First, they'll be coming at you two to one which you can handle. Second, you go to the gunfight with your sawed-off shotgun carried at port-arms and loaded with #3 Buckshot for close work, your pistol is your backup gun.

Third, you tell them that you are placing them under a citizen's arrest. Fourth, you give them a last chance to put their hands up. Lastly, you point your shotgun at them and give them the final warning—if they go for their guns, they will die."

"As soon as you see anyone go for his gun, shoot between the two men in front of you and fire off both barrels. There won't be any outlaws standing once the smoke clears. If they come at you with six men, I recommend that you fire at two separate outlaws instead of firing both barrels."

"It's unfortunate, but that is frequently the outcome of outlaws wanted dead or alive. These are the men that will face a hanging if brought in alive, so they have nothing to lose by trying to kill you."

This class brought them to lunch. The entire afternoon was spent mastering the ambush scenario.

<u>The Safe Arrest.</u> "This is a very common duty for a security agency. The local sheriffs need

experienced men to conduct arrests with a show of force. If done properly, you won't be in any danger. The key is to maintain control of the situation. Let's describe a classic situation. *The local sheriff has a court ordered arrest warrant to serve. This gang of three men killed an unarmed man for cheating at cards. The problem is that several witnesses saw the shooter throw a 'belly gun' on the floor after shooting him."*

"So, you and your partner step in the saloon with your sawed-off shotguns drawn. The lead man steps up to the table where the three men are sitting. The back up man puts his back to the wall next to the entrance door. The lead man orders the three men to stand up. As they stand, he yells out for everyone else to clear out, except the bartender. With everyone outside, the lead man orders the bartender to close the nighttime doors over the batwing doors. The bartender is then told to stand in front of the bar where he can't get to his shotgun in the back of the bar. Once it's clear that the outlaws won't be drawing their pistols,* *the bartender is then told to apply handcuffs to each man, locked behind their back."*

"It's a simplification, but the key features are that the lead man always had verbal control, the bartender was kept neutral, and the backup man was there if needed. If shooting starts, the backup man would be busy."

"Why not pistols in a close area instead of shotguns?"

"Just imagine how intimidating it is to look in the barrel of a sawed-off shotgun at six feet. It's enough to cut a man in half or decapitate him. Your job is to arrest them alive if possible. That shotgun helps to achieve that goal, my opinion. I also follow this method when I enter an outlaw's campsite."

<u>Transporting prisoners.</u> "This sound like a ridiculous subject, but it isn't. Any prisoner will try to escape and usually by killing you. Each man will carry two neck collars attached to a chain which can be padlocked to a tree or a stirrup. Plus, each man will carry two handcuffs. It's a serious matter transporting

killers, and every precaution should be taken. At all times, their hands are handcuffed in the back, not the front."

"What do you do if they need to relieve themselves?"

"One man stands guard with his pistol drawn, the other unarms himself, secures the chain to a tree or a saddle, and removes the handcuffs to allow nature's call. If there is any attempt to escape, he is shot dead on the spot."

"What do we do if we are alone."

"You let them relieve themselves in their britches!"

<u>Max as your partner.</u> "I save this section for last. There will be times when your partner will be my dog, Max. If the assignment is within ten miles, he can walk next to your horse. Otherwise, use a packhorse with the dog saddle for him to ride on. Max can assist you in everything but shooting your guns. He can be your backup on serving processes, he can track, he can smell an ambush, he can be your guard at camp, he will attack or kill on command, he

can make any outlaw answer questions after a few bites of flesh, and he has more common sense than most outlaws. Remember, he needs a lot of meat and beef jerky on assignments. Make friends with him the first chance you meet, and he'll be loyal to you forever."

"Last, let's review the personal accessories you need: the shotgun/45-70 slide, a compass, a set of 50X Binoculars, cervical collars/chains, padlocks, handcuffs, sewing kit with alcohol, and an awl."

"Oh yes, we all know about the 'awl.'"

"The last item to cover is writing your reports. After completing an assignment, you need to write a statement about the events. I want you to always follow this outline. It will keep your reports concise, organized, and to the point."

After many days of short meetings to answer their questions, the men continued to practice their shooting skills until Cal was satisfied that they were ready for their first assignment.

With the month at an end, Clarence and Floyd went to town to look for an apartment or a house to rent and then went back to get their families. Larry and Jim went straight to Boulder, quickly returned with their personal belongings, and took residence in the crop farm bunkhouse. With nothing to do till Clarence and Floyd returned, they started to work for Roger who had started the spring work.

***

A week later Cal and Clara were sitting by the fire after JR went to bed. Cal said, "looking back, it's been a very dynamic year."

Clara added, "let's follow the chronological order to the present."

"Ok, I guess it all started with my time with Amos Farley when I learned the bounty hunting trade. After being on my own for a while, I was referred to Capt. Ennis by Wayne Swanson. As a special Deputy Marshal, I had several significant assignments that built up my victim fund. Then I found you and while protecting you we fell in love. Our wedding was the next major landmark."

Clara took over, "then came the Whitehouse

capers which you miraculously managed to resolve. Yet, how we managed to survive the several assassination attempts will puzzle me forever."

Cal thought, "I believe that the major events this year were the development of the sheep and crop farms. We now have a huge flock of sheep and a crop enterprise that has gone commercial. Most important, we have two capable men that can run each farm."

Clara interjected, "you have built your victim fund to a self- sufficient level and you have helped several victims as well as several local people with their credit."

"Yes, and I've trained four good men to be independent as security agents. But most important, we have been blessed with the birth of our son."

Cal hesitated and finally said, "we are so fortunate, and I wonder what the future will bring. Thanks to God's blessing, we are certainly experiencing the American dream, heh."

***

EPILOGUE

Over the next years, Clara gave birth to two more children. The second child was a girl named Gloria. The third and last child was another boy named Griffin. During their upbringing, all three kid's interests became clear. By the time they finished their 10th grade all three were sent off to college to get an education in their field of interest.

CJ was a farmer at heart. He loved horses and the implements used in crop farming. It was a matter of time before he would take over the crop farm. Two years in an Agricultural and Business school prepared him for this responsibility.

Gloria loved all small animals, especially lambs. She didn't skip over the chores and learned the trade from Pedro. Going to an Agricultural and Business school was also her fate. It was no surprise when she fell in love with one of Pedro's sons and married. Cal and

Clara were proud to give the sheep farm's reins to her.

Griffin was a gun lover from the start. At an early age, he learned the proper fast draw technique, as well as the accuracy with a rifle and shotgun. At the young age of sixteen, he started accompanying the detectives on processes and prisoner transfers. By age eighteen he started going with his dad to serve arrest warrants. His first shootout was when he was twenty and had to kill his first outlaw who was going to kill his partner, Clarence Simpson. Griffin knew he would not go to an Agricultural school and thought he could avoid more schooling., but when dad said he was going to a different school to learn law and business management, Griffin resigned himself to two more years in the books. When Cal retired, Griffin took over the agency and added private investigations for unsolved murders.

The crop farm utilized 600 cultivated acres. Alfalfa became their primary product. It was in demand with sheep and dairy cows for milk production. The production yield was maximized with the use of a county ag agent, soil testing, commercial fertilizers, and seed selection for the climate and soil type.

The most important change to the crop enterprise was growing the market and cutting down expenses. The demand was there throughout the state via the railroad. Access to the railroad was the costly issue in money and time. The solution came when a railroad executive approved the construction of a side rail next to the crop farm. Enclosed boxcars were kept on the side rail for either crops or wool—year-round. The executive order had been approved by Samuel Whitcomb, a grateful voice from the past Rainbow Affair.

The sheep farm grew to a flock of 3000 sheep. Thanks to the cultivation and rotating pastures, the wool produced had a guaranteed market. The problem was the meat market was not growing with the times. The solution came when canning with tin cans became a popular item. With the beef and mutton available, a cannery opened in town with its own slaughter house. This brought the value of each animal to above market prices since the demand exceeded the supply.

The last improvement to service such a large flock was the development of electrically powered shears. Along with an abundance of experienced seasonal workers, the shearing crunch was brought under control. The last addition to the sheep farming industry was the new veterinarian in town. This vet had specialized in sheep biology and diseases. He proved to nearly eradicate lambing mortality and fleece quality related diseases.

Over the years, the symbiotic relationship between the crop and sheep farm became very important. The winter feed of alfalfa was at a discounted rate since it came from next door. The implements and manpower to cultivate the sheep farm also came from next door—again discounted. The need for extra workers during harvest time also provided access to workers from the sheep farm.

The security agency was the apparent "albatross" in the mix. In actuality, it provided relief for Cal who was still a bounty hunter at heart. Right from the start, Cal's reputation lead to requests for arrests from county and state agencies. The outlaw gangs were still over running the state. With the office in town, next to the railroad and telegraph, Cal and his men could get to a statewide location the next day. Getting quick results was their best advertisement. Of course, the newspaper exaggerated articles did not hurt either.

By the time Cal and Clara were ready to retire, the three kids took over the three divisions. Because to the hustle and bustle of the farms, they elected to move into town. Yet, when the need for help arose, both would ride back to the farm for a work or babysitting day.

At their combined retirement and 40th wedding anniversary, Cal made a short speech. "We were raised in the 70's, came to maturity and marriage in the late 80's, developed our businesses in the 90's and expanded them over the years to now, the 20th century. As entrepreneurs we took chances and made errors—but remember you cannot make an imprint on the times without trial and error, our way, heh!"

***

The End

Printed in the United States
By Bookmasters